RIVER
OF SOULS

T.L. BODINE

TREPIDATIO
PUBLISHING

ISBN: 978-1-950305-01-8 (sc)
ISBN: 978-1-950305-02-5 (ebook)
Library of Congress Control Number: 2019942177

First printing edition: August 23, 2019
Printed by Trepidatio Publishing in the United States of America.
Cover Design and Layout: Mikio Murakami
Interior Layout: Lori Michelle
Edited by Scarlett R. Algee
Proofread by Sean Leonard

Trepidatio Publishing, an imprint of JournalStone Publishing
3205 Sassafras Trail
Carbondale, Illinois 62901

Trepidatio books may be ordered through booksellers or by contacting:
Trepidatio | www.trepidatio.com
or
JournalStone | www.journalstone.com

DEDICATION:

For Andrew, who inspired me to start.
And for Angel, who made sure I finished.

RIVER
OF SOULS

CHAPTER ONE

WHEN THE DEAD first began to rise, people thought it was a miracle.

The first person to come back was just 19, a little younger than I was at the time. He'd killed himself with a shotgun blast to the chest and was pronounced dead at the scene. No one—not the paramedics, not the family who found the body—could have mistaken him for a survivor, not with all the bits of meat tangled by buckshot inside his chest cavity.

So not quite 12 hours later, imagine their surprise when he woke in the morgue, gasping and gurgling as he tried to speak. Imagine his family's confusion giving way to delight and hope. *Our sweet little boy is back*, someone probably said. *We have a second chance to make everything right.*

That's what I assume, anyway. The news never really said. Before they had a chance to run with the story, to book his family on all the morning talk shows or start up a bidding war for the rights to his memoir, the next corpse had awoken. And the next, and the next, and soon this wasn't a human interest piece anymore, not a freak accident or a miracle.

It was an epidemic.

"I'm not saying these people—these Undead—are dangerous . . . "

The radio's disembodied voice carries in the silence of the gas station. The radio itself sits on the counter, nestled between displays of lottery tickets and Bic lighters. One of the speakers is going out, so it crackles, but the sound is clear enough regardless. If you keep the volume low, you hardly notice it.

"I'm just saying, we still don't know what they really are. What they're capable of."

"They're sick," another person on the radio is saying. *"What you're suggesting, would you say that about a cancer patient? Someone with a chronic illness?"*

It's a hot night, sultry with late-summer humidity, and the air conditioner is broken. It's been broken for days, but the owner can't be fucked to care. He's not the one who has to work here, after all. The customers, when they come, are fleeting; they visit just long enough to pay for their gas or pick up a six-pack. Nobody's here long enough to notice the heat. Nobody except for me, anyway, and when you're working the graveyard shift at a 24-hour Kwik-Gas, you're in no position to bargain.

"Oh, come on, Marlene. You have to admit there's a difference between a chronic illness and someone who can walk around with half their guts spilling out without feeling it—"

I've got the front door open, propped by a crate of Pepsi 2-liters. The light outside flickers, and I can hear its intermittent buzz, the song of crickets out in the dark. Otherwise, it's quiet outside; it's been quiet for hours.

Los Ojos is a sleepy town, a wide spot in the highway, a town with more dive bars than schools. Nighttime customers are rare. We get truckers occasionally, but the overnighters usually stop a few miles down the highway at the Flying J, where they can take advantage of coin-op showers that charge by the minute or order a cup of coffee from some tired middle-aged waitress. Or else they make it a little way farther out of town, staying the night at the Indian casino resort about 40 minutes past on the interstate, sipping beers on the clock and feeding their paychecks through the slot machines.

On hot, quiet nights like this, it's easy to believe that you're the only person left in the world. It's easy to imagine that the sun will rise in a few hours and the streets will stay empty, the windows will stay shuttered, the doors will stay locked and still. That the desert will reclaim the town, and Los Ojos will go feral with its abandonment, like the aftermath of Armageddon.

But that won't happen.

Here in a few hours, once we've passed through the quiet time, the sun will come up and people will awaken and the lights will come on. Everyone will get back to their jobs, and life will keep on going, because we've missed our apocalypse; the zombies are here, but instead of tearing down civilization, they're standing in line at the Social Security office, waiting for their checks like everyone else.

My 16-year-old sister, Zoe, is lounging by the drink cooler. She's got the door propped open and is half-leaning inside, eyes closed behind her thick-framed glasses.

"Can you not?" I ask mildly, and not for the first time. "You're letting the cold out."

"Actually," she says, "there's no such thing as cold; just an absence of heat. You can't really let cold out so much as you let heat in. Thermodynamics and shit."

"Fine. You're letting the heat in, then." I peer over the counter at her. "Either way. You'll run up the electric bill."

She shrugs, but straightens and withdraws from the cooler. She pulls out a soda on the way. "Can you comp me one of these?"

I nod in agreement and tap in the appropriate code into the register. Foam bubbles over the top as she opens the tab, and she quickly covers the frothing opening with her mouth, taking in a long gulping drink before foam can spill out onto the linoleum. She finishes with a hiccup, grimacing, the now mostly-empty can half-crumpled. She wipes her hand, sticky with brown droplets, on the hem of her t-shirt.

"Very smooth."

She responds with a middle finger and a smirk. She slides

3

down against the glass, folding herself up on the floor, and digs a book out of her backpack. It's titled *Carnal Jesus: Understanding the Miracle of the Resurrection in Light of the Undead Awakening.* On the floor next to it, where it spilled out of her bag, is a book titled *Secrets of Lazarus: What Do We Really Know About the Reanimation Virus?*

Ever since our dad came back from the dead, Zoe's been reading anything she can get her hands on about the Undead. Books. Blogs. Podcasts. She lives and breathes Undead news. I guess it gives her some kind of peace, some kind of closure. I don't get it, but I'm not about to try and stop her. Getting between Zoe and something she's passionate about is like trying to get food away from a hungry, angry bear. It's always easier to just let her interests burn out, let them run their course, and eventually she'll get bored and look for something else to bury herself in. Assuming that dead people coming back to life is something you can get bored with.

I'm sure as fuck over it, myself.

Our mom died four years ago. She at least had the courtesy to stay dead. Then again, four years ago, everyone did.

At the end, she went down like some kind of wheezing cyborg, hooked up to the hospital machines. She'd been running from cancer for 20 years, in and out of remission. When it came back the last time, the only way she could destroy it was to take it down with her. That's how I like to imagine her, anyway: like some kind of comic book hero fighting a villain who can only be destroyed through self-sacrifice. It's a child's image, a stupid fantasy, but it's the way I like to remember her.

I dropped out of college to help out when Mom got sick the last time. There was a lot to do, and Dad couldn't handle it all on his own, so I stepped up and I helped because Zoe still needed to get to school, and bills still needed to be paid, and doctors had to be dealt with, and Dad was about as useful as a sack of shit.

So I moved back home for a little while and hoped it would get better, and every day I came a little closer to realizing that it never would.

Mom died, and I handled the funeral, and Dad still couldn't keep it together. So I stayed, each month thinking: *Just a little longer. He'll pull it together. This is just a temporary thing.*

It wasn't. It still isn't.

Mom had been dead a little over a year when the zombie thing started happening. It's one of those things you think will never happen to you, something that only happens in other towns, to other families. At the time, we were all too busy with the day-to-day bullshit of our lives to pay that much attention to anything, even corpses waking up in morgues, even the Undead Registration Act getting passed, the national debates about the rights of people who were probably not even really people anymore.

So I guess, in that sense, I didn't see it coming.

Dad's drinking had been picking up speed slowly over the last decade. As Mom's cancer ebbed and flowed, his drinking intensified; her disease went into remission, but his didn't. It'd been a constant for most of Zoe's life. By the time the cancer came back for the last time, Dad was already a functional alcoholic. Once Mom was in the ground, he wasn't really functional anymore. He picked up a prescription drug habit along the way, too, wheedling doctors here and there for an oxy to dull whatever new phantom pain he'd come up with that week, trading beers for pills at the local dive bar.

He'd go through brief periods of sobriety, ambitious turn-your-life-around attempts to fix all of the problems in his life, before he'd get crushed by the weight of them and turn right back to the bottle. He's always been like that: hot or cold, all or nothing.

Two years ago, I came home from the store, arms full of grocery bags, and everything was unusually quiet when I came in the house. Late afternoon sun streamed through the window, dust hanging suspended in the beam. The stillness felt heavy, suffocating, like a house that had been shut up for a long time. The house smelled like liquor and vomit.

It was the silence that tipped me off. It wasn't uncommon to see Dad motionless on the couch, but this time he wasn't snoring. The absence of sound filled the room.

Something about his position was all wrong. He was lying on the couch, but at an uncomfortable angle, like he'd fallen into it and couldn't be bothered to adjust his position. I edged closer and saw the wide-open eyes, the glassy expression, the froth of vomit crusting his lips. I saw the discoloration, the blue ashiness of his dark skin, and knew that he was dead.

I wasn't surprised.

Afterward, people tried to convince me that I was. The paramedics, the social worker, the lawyer who would eventually handle the details of his disability pension after his resurrection—all of them tried to comfort me through my "shock." The shock, they said, was why I hadn't cried. It was why I hadn't grieved.

I might have had a chance to cry, if he'd stayed dead longer. I might have been able to grieve if he'd given me the opportunity. But at the time, all I felt was a hollowness, and before that empty place could fill with sorrow, I was getting a call from the morgue, and then I was talking to a lawyer and filing paperwork and stitching together an income from his disability payments and my part-time job. My days have been swept up in taking care of him, making sure he takes his medication, keeping him from wandering out after curfew or venturing into places where the Undead have been forbidden.

I still haven't cried for him. I have a hard time believing I ever will.

Time is relative, and it's never quite as relative as when you're stuck somewhere you don't want to be. The hours creep past agonizingly slowly, time stretching out between them like gum left on a hot sidewalk.

The heat at last begins to relent around 3 A.M. With the front door to the store still open, the cold starts to drift in, or the heat starts to drift out—however that works. It's almost bearable, anyway.

Zoe's restless. She keeps shifting from her seated position against the drink cooler to lying sprawled on her stomach, mass of curly hair spilling over her shoulders as she bends over an open book. Back to her feet, pacing the aisle, browsing snack foods with a disinterested expression before returning, resigned, to her reading. Her glasses keep slipping down her nose, slick with sweat.

Zoe's short and built like our mom, all rounded edges and plump features. She hates it. She wishes she were gaunt and angular and exotic-looking, like she'd gotten the cheekbones Dad and I share. She used to say as much, when she was younger and it wasn't weird to talk about your insecurities with your big brother.

These days, it seems like she doesn't talk to me about much of anything. Not since Mom and Dad died. She's always busy, closed off in another world, always reading or locked away in her room, working on whatever project has captured her attention. Doing whatever it is she does these days, and doing it without me.

Not that I can blame her for keeping secrets, not when I have a few of my own.

First secret: Zoe has no idea how close she is to being taken away.

When Dad came back from the dead, there were so many people to meet with, doctors and social workers to talk to, paperwork to sign. It wasn't like the chaos after Mom's death: the hours spent choosing flower arrangements and caskets, the time spent accepting the apologies of mourners. It was a colder, more detached sort of chaos, a bureaucratic gauntlet like buying a house.

First, the doctors had to confirm that Dad was, in fact, a member of the Undead. There are legal designations to draw between those who had been legally dead—heart stopped—and brought back from the brink, and those who had been truly dead—brain activity halted and reactivated after a significant delay, biological processes permanently altered—and resurrected as Undead. The doctors have to examine you and sign off on everything to make sure you're dead enough to count.

Then the paperwork started, the meetings with suits. Signing waivers to show we understood the changes in Dad's rights now that he was a member of the Undead. Obtaining his Undead identification card, which would allow him to gather his meager disability pension and give him a standing prescription for Lazarus, the life-extension drug that all the Undead rely on to maintain their humanity. That part's non-negotiable: if you're Undead, you take your drugs, and you go to your monthly doctor's appointments to make sure you're not going to be a public health threat.

Kind of ironic, honestly, seeing as prescription drugs got him into this mess to begin with. But the alternative is worse: you go off your Lazarus and you lose that human part of yourself, the part that thinks and feels and remembers. All that's left is anger, and hunger, and the impossible strength of people who can't feel pain anymore.

So, all right. I can see the value in staying on your meds.

Anyway. I was talking about Zoe.

Somewhere in the middle of the rest of the suits I had to meet with, there was a social worker who was supposed to be helping us with "this difficult life transition." I didn't catch his name, or else I've forgotten it in the two years since I met him, but I'll always remember the way his face looked when he pulled me out onto the front porch.

Zoe was with Dad in the living room, sitting on the couch sharing a movie in silence, her head on his chest like a little girl, like nothing had happened, like everything was fine and normal. I closed the door behind us and met the social worker's gaze. He was pretty young, maybe in his 30s, and he had a look in his eyes that I recognized from staring into the mirror: the look of a guy who's taken on too much, but can't abandon it now. Maybe that was why he bothered pulling me aside at all; maybe he recognized the look of a kindred spirit and felt compelled to say something about it.

I lit a cigarette for myself and offered him one. He declined.

"You're young," the social worker said. "I want you to take that into account when you make your decision. It's not selfish to need a break. It might be the best thing for you."

I stayed silent, quietly nursing the cigarette as I waited for him to get to the point.

"You understand that your father is no longer entitled to many of the rights he once had."

I nodded. That was thanks to the Undead Registration Act, which had passed just a few months earlier.

"Even if he were capable, which I think you and I both know he's not, he wouldn't be able, legally, to assume custody of a minor." His gaze strayed toward the door, indicating the living room beyond. "I understand you're the only family?"

I nodded. There were some others—a cousin, maybe, or an aunt in another state—but none we had contact with, and certainly none who would take in a teenager they'd never met. None had come to Mom's funeral.

"There's no shame in getting help from the state, Mr. Montoya."

I grimaced at the title. That wasn't my name; it was my father's, a badly-sized hand-me-down. But the social worker either didn't notice, or decided to pretend to ignore it, and I let him. He left me with a pamphlet, a business card tucked up inside, and promised to be back to check in on how our "transition" was going. It was all kept very courteous, very professional, but I could read through the subtext easily enough: I was Zoe's last living relative, her guardian, the last line of defense between her and foster care.

The social worker was expecting me to fuck that up. And if I did, he'd be waiting to step in. How fucking courteous.

⌒

Back in the present, Zoe has given up on her reading once again and has resumed pacing through the aisles.

I watch her, feeling a rise of anxiety: a twisting, gutted feeling. I need to talk to her, but every time I start to open my mouth, she shifts position or turns away and I lose my nerve. I may have been forced into this role as breadwinner, this surrogate father position, but I'm no good at it. I'm too much of a coward. I worry too much about her liking me, about seeming cool.

Secret number two I'm keeping from her: this letter I got two days ago. I've read it over enough times that I practically have it memorized now:

Mr. Davin Montoya,

We are writing to you today to extend an invitation to our inpatient Undead treatment program.

We understand that your father, Ignacio Montoya, has been a registered Undead for 18 months. Based upon the information provided by his physician through mandatory reporting, we believe that he would be an ideal candidate for our innovative new treatment program. For more information, or to schedule a tour of our premises, please reach us at the number and address below.

I haven't called them yet.

I've been telling myself that I'd ask Zoe her opinion first. I've been pretending that I could get her on my side, and we could go talk to Dad together and explain to him what we've decided. It's a nice fantasy, this idea that we might be able to send him to some treatment facility and not have to worry about him every day.

Not worry about whether or not he gets his Lazarus doses on time.

Not worry about leaving Zoe home alone with him, just in case.

It's such a nice fantasy that I don't want to risk destroying it with real life, because I know Zoe won't agree to it.

My shift ends at 6 A.M. Zoe's asleep in the break room, curled up on the small loveseat the night shift had once salvaged from behind a dumpster. It's a nice couch, lumpy and time-worn, and—like the radio by the cash register—something the general manager is best not knowing about.

"Hey." I prod Zoe's shoulder. "It's time to get up."

She grunts and mutters something unintelligible.

Across the break room, my relief is stashing her bag in a locker. She's a tall, thin girl with hair cut into a faux-hawk, shaved up one side and combed over the other. She's wearing the blue polo and black pants we're supposed to wear on the job. When she moves, her pants leg lifts to reveal pink leopard-pattern socks. Her name is Jo, and she's probably my closest friend.

We know almost nothing about each other.

"Problems at home again, huh?" Jo asks, nodding at Zoe's sleepy figure.

"Yeah." I jab Zoe again, more forcefully this time, giving her shoulder a good shake.

"Tell me about it." Jo rolls her eyes. "When I was her age, I'd do anything to keep from having to stay home with *my* dad. She's lucky she can tag along with you. I had to find some place to be on my own, and let me tell you, I never made good choices."

I laugh, because I know she's expecting me to. Jo knows that our dad is an alcoholic. She doesn't know that he's a corpse. Somehow, the first detail had seemed easier to share, less vulnerable. It's proven to be a useful shorthand for explaining why I bring my sister to work so often, why I can't always pick up shifts or pull overtime.

It's something a lot of people in Los Ojos can relate to.

Zoe's finally made it upright, and is meditatively cleaning her glasses on the hem of her shirt. She sets them down in her lap and rubs at her eyes with the heels of her hands, trying to clear the sleep from them. With her hair sticking up in odd directions and the sleepy look on her face, she looks like a little kid. Sometimes I think I'm being too cautious, not wanting to leave her alone with Dad; but then I see her like this, small and vulnerable and childish, and a wave of protective instinct comes over me.

I never let him lay a hand on her when he was alive, no matter how wasted he got. I'll be damned if I let him hurt her now, walking dead or not.

"Have a good night, Jo," I say, even though it's nearly morning. Zoe finally puts on her glasses and grabs her backpack, slipping the strap over one shoulder and letting it hang against her side.

"You guys too," she says with a good-natured smile.

Outside, over the crest of the mesa, the sun is threatening to rise. It lingers on the horizon, pale and hesitant, painting the clouds in shades of pink and lavender. The mesa stands against it in silhouette, a harsh crag of stone that overlooks Los Ojos. To the west there's the river, and beyond that, the reservation, the casino, the interstate and—eventually—Arizona. Just now, the town's starting to wake up, the earliest morning traffic starting to nose its way out onto the main roads, and the town comes alive like a flower lifting its face to the sun.

Time for me to go to bed. Dad may be the walking corpse in the family, but I'm the one keeping a schedule like a vampire.

CHAPTER TWO

I'M EXHAUSTED BY the time I get home. Zoe shuffles inside and down the hall without speaking, offering a vague grunt by way of "good night." I'm eager to do the same, but I have to tend to Dad first.

The master bedroom is on one side of the hall, sharing a wall with the hall bathroom. Our bedrooms are on the opposite side, so that my bedroom door opens nearly parallel to his. After Zoe disappears into her room, closing the door behind her, I stop outside Dad's room and listen for sounds coming from inside. Silence; no movement inside, not even a snore. Even though I do this every day, anxiety still clutches at me as I reach to twist the knob.

Taking care of Dad would be one thing if he were still just a drunk caught in the selfish jaws of his depression. That was difficult to manage, but something we'd grown accustomed to. Working around Dad's disease was something I'd learned to fold into the fabric of my life, starting as far back in childhood as I can remember, and the dysfunctional rhythms of it were all familiar, comforting in some twisted way. How to gauge his mood, how to tiptoe around his bouts of explosive temper.

The problem is that, in death, he's the same man he's always been. But he's also an Undead, which comes with its own set of rules.

For a while, when the Reanimation Event was still fresh news, the Undead tried to return to their normal lives. At first, people tried to pretend that the Undead weren't even really dead at all, like it was just some kind of disease, some kind of fluke. Mostly dead, or formerly-presumed-dead, but not Undead; that chasm between living and dead gapes wide, and there's a lot of things to fill that moat. If someone's just sick—if something terrible has happened to someone, but they're still fundamentally alive—then they're just like anyone else. They can work and get married and raise kids and get on with their lives.

But if you're dead, that all changes. Undeath isn't pretty. It isn't miraculous. You don't come back clean and whole; you come back bearing the scars of whatever killed you, and they never heal. Undead bodies don't regenerate. They don't feel pain, either, or get tired, and bodies that no longer have the limitations of pain are capable of doing amazing, terrible things.

Lazarus is supposed to fix all of that.

It's an injection, some cocktail of steroids and hormones and God knows what else; I don't know exactly what's in it. But it eases some of the symptoms of being Undead, slows the decay process, keeps people from rotting away to bone and sinew. It keeps their minds from slipping, allows them to retain their humanity. It stops them from becoming true zombies: vicious, bloodthirsty, missing a higher consciousness.

The consequences of going without the drug have become the stuff of urban legend. Supposedly, a woman once went off Lazarus and went crazy; she tore long strips of skin off her own face and ate her young daughter, who was asleep in her bed. The story goes that she started at the little girl's toes so she could hear her screaming. When they found the lady, they say, she had plucked out her own eyes and was suckling them in her mouth like a pair of candies.

Another time, the story goes, a little baby died in his crib and came back, hours later. His family couldn't bear to think that he had really died, that he was really Undead, so they refused to register him, refused to give him his Lazarus. They say he climbed out of his crib, super strong, and crawled up into his parents' bed at night to tear at them with his little fingers and sharp milk teeth. They say he tore out his mother's guts while she slept, one tiny toddler-sized fistful of flesh after another.

14

The stories are probably bullshit.

But what we know for sure is that sometimes, Undead lose themselves, and they can do bad things.

"Hey, Dad."

He doesn't answer, so I push the door open.

Since he's not stuck on the graveyard shift, Dad's bedroom is the only one in the house without blackout curtains. Early morning light trickles in through his window and illuminates the room with a grayish haze, that weird twilight that makes everything seem a little bit fake. In the dim light, I make out my father sitting up in bed, staring intently at a blank patch of wall. I hesitate, trying to get a feel for his mood, trying to understand what's going through his head before I come in. He doesn't look up or acknowledge me.

He looks a lot like me: tall, thin, with prominent bone structure. He's gaunter now that he's been dead for a while, and his cheekbones jut up sharply over the hollows of his cheeks; his dark eyes are sunken a little beneath his brows. His skin, once dark and coppery, is grayed now, ashy and bloodless, a stark contrast against his dark hair. Perched up in bed the way he is, he looks like some kind of gargoyle, some grotesque scarecrow meant to frighten away the birds.

"Dad . . . ?"

"What did I tell you." He speaks with flat intonation; it's not a question, but rather a statement. "Boy, what did I tell you about the rats."

"Rats?"

His eyes turn, then, to meet mine; even in the semi-dark of his slowly brightening room, they look wide and bloodshot.

"The rats in the walls. What did I *tell you* about the fucking rats? All night I've been hearing them scratching and chewing the wires. Listen."

I listen, but I know there are no rats. It's a delusion, alcohol-related psychosis.

You know what they say: once a drunk, always a drunk. In my dad's case, that's literally true. He's never sobered up, and I don't think he ever can; he's caught in some kind of perpetual inebriation, some stasis where his mind oscillates between intoxication and withdrawal. I wonder, sometimes, if the Lazarus isn't an unnecessary cruelty, if forcing his mind to stay intact in this state is actually worse than letting his consciousness slip away. But I'm too afraid of what might happen to seriously consider letting him skip a dose.

"It's time for your medicine," I tell him, ignoring his comments about the rats.

He fixes me with a hard, mean stare, but his focus is unsteady, as if he's looking through me.

I move past the foot of his bed and into the bathroom. It's dusty and cobwebby; he has no need of it anymore. The only area that gets much use is the medicine cabinet, and I reach for that, nudging it open and pulling out a glass vial filled with a yellow-green liquid, and a fresh syringe. This I unwrap and load, hands moving by muscle memory from doing this so often. When I emerge back into the room, Dad's pulled away from the edge of the bed and is huddled against the wall, hugging bony knees to his chest.

"Don't," he begs, and the tonality of his voice has shifted away from the flat affect of before.

When his dark eyes meet mine this time, there's a light in them, understanding or clarity. I wish he wouldn't. It's easier to deal with him when I can pretend he doesn't know anything that's happening; these flashes of lucidity are the worst. They remind me of better times, times we're never going to have again.

"Please." He cringes from me as I approach. "Don't. I don't want it."

I ignore him, grabbing for an arm. I grasp it, twist, pull it against my body to brace it into place so he won't squirm. Pinch thick fingerfuls of flesh from his bicep and jab the needle into the tissue. Am grateful, as always, that Lazarus goes into the muscle and not the vein; I can't imagine trying to hit him with any more accuracy than this.

As the medicine leaves the syringe and flows into his body, Dad lets loose a sound like a wounded animal—half wail, half snarl, mixed with curses. I jump back, instinctively avoiding the fist that swings at me, and the needle tears at his arm as I tug it free. Blood, thick and blackish and oozing like gelatin, creeps toward the torn space in his arm, but I'm more focused on the other arm; his fingers brush past my face, yellowed fingernails like claws threatening to tear into my skin. He lunges for me, and I dart away from him, diving for the open door. I make it through just in time, slamming it shut behind me. I hear Dad slam against it, pounding his fists on the wood.

"You son of a bitch!" he yells, and I hear him clawing at the door as I lock it up, hanging the key back on the wall next to it.

I go into the kitchen, pull out a Tupperware, drop the used syringe into it. It's not a sharps container, but it'll do. I don't want to go back into the room, not when I can still hear my dad wailing on the other side of the door. Later, when I'm awake, I'll unlock it, let him come out to watch TV for a while or go for a walk outside while the sun's still out, before the curfew kicks in. But for now, I need to know that he's contained so I can get some sleep.

The sun's fully risen outside, and the yellow glow of it leaks in around the blackout curtains. I collapse into bed, not bothering to get undressed, and fall asleep against the distant thumping on my father's door, his furious wails.

"This can't be happening."

That was a common refrain when all of this started. Faced with the reality of the dead coming back to life, people were initially shocked and skeptical. Maybe they weren't really dead. Maybe it was just media hysteria blowing things out of proportion. Maybe the whole thing was faked, some kind of jumbled conspiracy.

And maybe, for the people who got the benefit of watching it all unfold in the abstract, that could all seem true. It's easy to poke holes in a story on TV. It's easy to scoff and pull apart the plot threads of a story, even a story that the teller swears is true.

But when it's actually happening to you? When it's someone you know? When it affects your life? You don't get the luxury of pretending that none of it is real. You just have to accept it, the way our species has accepted every other impossible-but-true fact: the size of the universe, the composition of atoms, the motion of light, the unlikely biology of the platypus. When it's happening and it's in front of you, you no longer get to say "this can't be real," even if you have no way of understanding it.

And when it's your life that's been turned upside down—when you're the one staring at the blinking, talking corpse of your father—you don't get to waste time wondering about the "why" and "how" and trying to make sense of things. You just pick up where you are, and you deal.

And that's what we've been doing for two years now. Dealing. It's not easy. It's definitely not glamorous. But we've found a sort of routine, fallen into a rhythm.

It's amazing what you can adapt to.

When I sleep, I dream—as I often do—about death.

The nightmares started just before Mom died, when the looming specter of her death was inevitable. Considering everything that was going on, it's probably not that surprising that death would haunt my nightmares. Dreams are supposed to be your brain's way of making sense of things, processing, letting go, taking out the trash from your subconscious. I guess when you keep having the same dream over and over, that's got to mean you have a lot of garbage to sort through.

It's been four years, and though the dreams don't come every night as they once did, they're a regular enough visitor in my subconscious that I've developed a strange sort of familiarity with them. They're like old friends, strangely comforting in a way. Somehow, they no longer feel like nightmares.

In the dream, I'm standing on a small island of light, surrounded by darkness. The darkness ebbs and flows, like waves lapping at the shore of the beach, and with each cresting wave the ocean grows a little bigger, my island shrinking away. I know, standing in this diminishing spotlight, that soon the darkness will completely envelop me, and I'll cease to exist.

This was once terrifying. Now it's oddly comforting.

I face the darkness with longing. I want it to wash over me and pull me under to a place where nothing matters, a place where I don't have to worry about anything, a place where everything is silent and no decisions must be made.

But the darkness doesn't come for me. Instead, it's the dream that fades, and I'm left in the semi-darkness of my bedroom, hints of light creeping around the blankets I've hung over the windows to obscure the sun while I sleep around the graveyard hours.

The light has an aged, golden quality: midday sun. Beyond my door, I can make out the sounds of movement in the hall: Zoe stirring awake, perhaps, padding down to the hall bathroom to start a shower. From Dad's room, silence; I imagine him lurking beyond the door, cowering in his bed, holding vigil for rats that aren't there. I imagine the ugly gash in his arm, the torn edges of flesh from where the needle broke free this morning; a small tear, but one that will gape open forever, the unsealed wounds of a dead immune system. The image sends a shudder down my spine.

I need to get up. I need to cross the hall and unlock the door so Dad can come out for a while. He has TV shows he watches in the afternoon. It's cruel to leave him in there. He's a corpse, but he still takes pleasure in some things, even if he can't eat, or feel pain, or heal. Even if he won't get any better. Even if every day is going to be the same, for months and years, maybe forever; no one knows what happens in the end.

The Undead who've died a second time have done so violently, sometimes at the hands of law enforcement after losing themselves to the violence that lurks in their nature. Some have committed suicide. Many others have tried suicide and failed, going on to be horrifically deformed but still standing. There's an Undead who shares a doctor with Dad. I see him, sometimes, in the waiting room when we go in for the monthly Lazarus refills. His face is a red mess of meat and bone wrapped in bandages that keep the blood from seeping out through the sponge-like tissue. He tried to kill himself, the barrel of the gun pressed up into the hollow of his chin, but the bullet missed everything vital.

Every time I see him, I wonder whether he'll find the courage to try it again, or if he's resigned himself now to this fate. I wonder how it feels to be his caretaker, bending over to put saline drops in that one good eye of his, the lidless eyeball that stares unblinking from the bloody mess of his face. I wonder if he feels like a monster now that he looks like one.

I need to get up and tend to Dad, but I can't do it.

The letter from the Undead treatment facility is sitting, creased from multiple re-readings, on my dresser. The ceiling fan shifts the air in the room, and the edges of the paper flutter as if winking at me, politely demanding my attention.

I call the facility and set an intake appointment with them for Friday. I'm surprised at how they are on the phone: courteous but distant, businesslike. I ask, repeatedly, whether this really will be covered by the government, and the woman I talk to reassures me until I can hear the frustration creeping up at the edges of her voice.

It takes me three days to get up the courage to tell Zoe about the plan. By the time I do, it's already Thursday, and I can't put it off any longer. Dad's napping on the couch. Like an old dog, Dad sleeps a lot; it's one of the few pleasures left to the Undead, I guess. I try not to think about it; seeing him there, so deep in sleep that he's forgotten to breathe, a corpse lying prostrate beneath the sunny window, brings back memories of the day I found his body. Memories that make me feel cold and sick to contemplate.

I linger outside of Zoe's room. She's rigged a studio light to the outside of her door; it flashes red to let me know she's recording. From inside her room I can hear her voice, muffled but loud with projection.

"The mainstream media is trying to hide this video," she's saying, loud and clear, her on-camera voice. "And is it any wonder why? It's just one more example of an unarmed citizen being gunned down in the middle of the street—and all because of what? They've laid out arbitrary rules for when your rights end? I'm sorry, but unless we want to see a militarized police force that uniformly practices 'shoot first, ask questions later,' then we need to stand up and demand justice for the Undead."

She falls silent, and in the lull I hear the clicking of keys and a mouse button. I knock and wait. The light shuts off, and I take that as an invitation to come inside.

Zoe's taken an interest in web journalism, and the interest has consumed both her life and her bedroom. One half of her room is set up like the world's smallest film studio. She's got her computer hooked up to a webcam, which is set up opposite a homemade green screen hanging against the wall. On a different wall, she's got a corkboard covered with news clippings, push pins, and red string—conspiracy theory style—and there's usually a stack of books and loose papers overtaking the floor and bed and any other flat surface.

She's currently hunched over the computer keyboard, big headphones over both ears, studiously looking between her dual monitors. On one screen, there's a video editing program. On the other, multiple tabs opened to YouTube, news outlets, God knows what else.

I linger a moment, unsure if she's noticed me, not wanting to startle her.

"Yes?" she asks, without looking up from her work.

I gesture vaguely at her computer. "Please tell me you're not going to get us put on a list somewhere."

"Please, Davin. Give me some credit." She pulls the headphones off and sets them on her desk, leaning back to give me a disparaging look. "Just because you wouldn't know the first thing about flying incognito on the web doesn't mean I'm just as dumb. Besides, that's totally not important. Come here."

I do as she asks, moving to stand beside her. She points at one of the computer monitors. "Have you seen this?"

There's a headline from a local newspaper: UNREGISTERED UNDEAD FOUND AND CONTAINED; PUBLIC NO LONGER UNDER THREAT. The photograph they're running alongside looks like anybody else from Los Ojos: middle-aged, dark-haired, tanned skin, your classic New Mexico mutt. The photo's in black-and-white, which doesn't help with making him look any less corpse-like. The story itself is pretty short, just a couple of paragraphs telling the same type of narrative that these stories always do: an Undead was found on the loose, evading curfew; he wasn't registered with the proper authorities; attempts to subdue him ended in violence when he turned upon the police.

"Okay, you got that?" Zoe asks, watching my face intently as I scan over the story. "Because I'm about to blow your mind."

She clicks over to another tab, and there's a grisly photograph, a blurry still from a grainy video. It shows a body: blue button-up shirt, collar standing partially upright against a neck that's no longer holding up much of anything. In place of a head, there's a spatter of gore, red-black ooze and pink flecks of brain.

I flinch. You'd think the gross-out horror of living alongside a dead man for two years would give me a stronger stomach, but nobody's ever prepared to see something like that.

"Sorry. No pun intended." Zoe looks satisfied, though; there's a fierce, almost predatory gleam in her eyes, like a dog who's caught sight of a squirrel on the wrong side of a fence.

She clicks a button, and the still photograph disappears, replaced with a brief video. Dash cam footage, probably, but maybe caught by some nosy rubbernecker with a cell phone. It's the guy from the news story—that middle-aged guy who could practically have been our father—cornered by police in the alley between Dollar General and Smith's. Someone says something that the sound doesn't pick up, there's a series of pops and bangs, and then he's on the ground, most of his head splattered on the pavement.

The clip is too short to make out much context about the shooting, but it doesn't look like he was threatening them. If he was, he didn't get far.

"It sucks," I say, guardedly, because Zoe's staring at me with an expectant expression. "Who is he?"

"Was," she corrects me, with a patronizing look. "They didn't release a name. But from what I can see, it looks like he was unregistered, and buying Lazarus off the street. One source said he was shot during a drug bust. A different source says he had actually fled the scene and was pursued before the police caught up and shot him in cold blood."

The police developed their "shoot for the head" policy for the Undead pretty soon after the epidemic first started. It's a PR nightmare, but a logistical necessity. Being dead means losing nerve endings and pain signals. If you cut them, they bleed, but they might not notice or care about it. And without the limitations of pain, the body's instinctive avoidance of injury, you discover that you're capable of doing all sorts of things you'd never done before—feats of strength and stamina that would put any living Olympian to shame.

Cops realized pretty quickly that handcuffs aren't too effective when the criminals are willing and able to rip off their own hands at the wrist to escape them. They found out pretty fast that a double-tap to the chest with a pistol barely registers on a corpse's pain scale.

It only took a few nasty altercations before cops started training in more lethal methods. The police force took to it pretty readily. There have been a few decades of pop culture training, after all, about exactly what you're supposed to do with zombies. Any kid who's ever played a video game knows as much.

"That doesn't make any sense," I tell her. "Why would they shoot him? If he's buying Lazarus on the street somehow, he's still dosed up. He's not going to lose himself."

She nods at me. "Exactly my point."

"There's got to be more to it, though. Some reason he was unregistered to begin with. He's probably hiding something, or involved in something bad, and the Lazarus deal—if that even really happened—was just covering for it. You know how stories get garbled."

"I can't believe you don't care." Zoe's eyes go wide, comically enlarged by her thick glasses. Her nostrils flare, indignant. "How can you be like 'oh, it doesn't matter, oh, they were asking for it.' What if this were Dad? What if it were *me*?"

"I didn't say I don't care," I say, but something's churning uncomfortably in my gut and I'm trying really hard not to imagine Zoe's brains splattered across the pavement, black-framed glasses sitting in a puddle of gore. "I'm just saying, the Undead know the rules. If you're willing to break those rules, if you're willing to be a criminal, you have to be willing to accept the consequences."

"And a fair consequence is *death*?" Zoe gestures vaguely at the computer screen, shaking her head in disgust. Frizzy curls bob around her chin, tangling with the headphones currently resting around her neck. "He wasn't hurting anybody. He wasn't violent. The media can say all it wants that the Undead are dangerous, but that just doesn't line up with the facts."

" . . . Zoe, are you recording this?"

She pauses, eyes still wide behind her glasses, expression slack and blank—the same look she used to get when I'd catch her poking through my comic books and couldn't come up with a convincing lie about what she was doing in my room.

She quickly taps a button on the keyboard, halting the recording, and grins sheepishly. "Off the record, though. For real. Do you think the Undead are dangerous?"

I shrug. "I think anybody can be dangerous. Alive or dead, whatever race or gender or religion you are, there's always somebody out there capable of doing some fucked-up shit."

Her expression is exasperated, like I've missed the point entirely, but she doesn't immediately offer a rebuttal. Instead, she falls silent, turning her eyes back to the computer screen and clicking at video editing options, as if intent to look very busy.

"Anyway," I say, briskly, trying to shepherd the discussion to a new subject, "I actually didn't come in here to argue politics. I have something I need to tell you."

She doesn't look up. I hesitate, watching the back of her head, trying to tell if she's paying attention. This isn't how I wanted this to go, but there's no time to turn back now.

"I got an offer, a few days ago, to enroll Dad in a treatment program. I've called them, and it seems pretty legit."

The muscles in her back tense slightly; her head cocks to the side. She doesn't turn, but I know I have her attention.

"Anyway, it's inpatient treatment at a facility about an hour from here. He'd stay there, and they'd make sure he got his Lazarus and everything else, and we could go visit."

"Like a nursing home."

"Yeah. I guess." The idea sits uncomfortably in my head. It's not strange for two siblings to discuss putting a parent in a nursing home—and while that usually happens later in life, it's not completely absurd at our age. The idea is so normal, so banal, that it makes me uneasy. It's dangerously close to making sense, and no part of our life has made sense in years.

She turns to look at me, eyes narrowed shrewdly. "Does he know?"

"I haven't told him." I can't meet her eyes. "I think it's best, though. He could make friends, people like him. It'd be better than staying locked up in a bedroom half the day."

She laughs, and it's a mirthless, scoffing sound. That's the problem with little sisters: they can always see through your bullshit. "You just don't want to be responsible for him anymore." I start to respond, to refute this accusation, but before I can say anything, she interrupts, "It's okay. I can't blame you for that. You should still ask what he wants, though. He's a person. He's our *dad*."

25

"He thinks there are rats in the walls," I say, and the desperation in my voice gives me away, betrays my frustration. "The other day I went in there to give him his meds and he was tearing up the carpet looking for a hidden microphone. He's crazy."

She shrugs, giving me a hopeless sort of "I don't know what to tell you" look, and turns back to her computer. I think she's closed off the discussion, but instead I see that she's pulling up links about Undead treatment facilities. Pretty soon the screen is populated in websites.

"The Lazarus House," she reads aloud, clicking so rapidly between pages I have no idea how she can actually read them. "Huh. That's interesting. Looks like there's a half dozen or so of these inpatient treatment facilities that have opened up this year. Guess you're not the only person sick of dealing with a corpse in the family. Oh! Oh wow, this is so close to us, and it's the only one in the whole Southwest region." She pauses, nose wrinkling, and turns to look at me. "That's so weird. Why Los Ojos, New Mexico, of all places?"

I shrug. "It's at the old Spanish mission," I say, and then add blandly, "It looks nice."

"Huh. Yeah." More clicking and looking at things. I wait for her to speak again. "Is there a contract? Is he locked into this or anything?"

"I don't think so. They didn't say that. I'm pretty sure I can just go check him in and pick him up again later if he doesn't like it." I can't imagine he's going to like anything, but that makes it sound more hospitable.

"Well, that's cool at least." Click. Click. Scroll. "This is weird. Looks like all of these facilities are in shit towns. Eh. Property value thing, I guess. So when are you going?"

"Tomorrow."

Cold, icy silence for a moment. I'm waiting for her to blow up, but she's going to do the silent treatment instead. "You weren't going to tell me sooner?"

"I'm telling you now."

No response. Silence mode activated. She leans in closer to her computer, making a point of angling her shoulders away from me, shutting me down with her body language. I take the opportunity to retreat with the closest thing to a victory I'm likely to get.

CHAPTER THREE

FRIDAY AFTERNOON COMES earlier than I'd like. I'm
glad I don't have work tonight; sleeping today has been a
jumbled mess of half-sensible dreams and constant waking, and
by the time I dragged myself from bed and stumbled through the
motions of getting ready, I was more exhausted than if I'd just
stayed up. It's a little after 3:00 pm now, and Dad's intake is
scheduled for 5:00. I can't put it off.

He's on the couch when I enter the living room, watching some
reality show. He's cupping his elbow in his opposite hand,
fidgeting and picking at the loose edges of his wounded skin the
way you'd mess with a blister. The hole has gotten wider in the days
since, now a ragged gash that runs deep as well as wide. Glimpses
of white-streaked pink muscle show through the black goo.

"Stop that." Zoe's sitting next to him, legs curled up under
her, book in one hand, but she's not reading it. She looks
distracted even as her fingers curl over Dad's wrist. "Dad, stop.
You're hurting yourself."

"It doesn't hurt," he says, without taking his eyes from the
screen, fingertips still worrying at the edges of his torn flesh.
"That's weird. This should hurt, shouldn't it?"

This is why you're taking him to a facility, I think, steeling my
nerves as I approach. *The people there will be trained to deal with shit
like this.*

"Hey, Dad," I say, trying to sound cheerful. I overdo it, and
the words come out sounding false. Zoe's eyes lift up to mine,
brows raised in a skeptical quirk. I clear my throat and try again.
"Let's go for a drive. I want to talk to you about something."

We had a dog once, a little floppy-eared spaniel that someone had abandoned out on the highway. Just drove out, opened the passenger door, and dumped him on the side of the road. I imagine the conversation had gone similarly: *Come on, boy, let's go for a car ride!*

Dad turns to look at me, and the lucidity in his eyes breaks my heart. "I don't think I'm okay to drive. I think I'm a little drunk."

"It's okay. I'm DD." I look over his head, try to meet Zoe's eyes, but she's looking away. "Come on."

It takes a few minutes, but I manage to get him up and bundled into the car. I've packed his bag with a few changes of clothes and stowed it in the trunk; I'm not sure what he'll need, what the people at the facility will be expecting him to have. I guess I'll be finding out soon enough.

I leave him in the car with the engine going, so the air conditioner has a chance to start working, and pop back inside. Zoe's still sitting on the couch, staring at her book, but I notice that she hasn't turned the page since I first came into the living room. Her eyes are unfocused, expression introspective.

"You're welcome to come," I say. "But I'll understand if you want to stay."

"They won't let me come," she says, without looking up. "I'm a minor. Didn't you read their website?"

"Uh . . . "

"You have to make special arrangements to visit the premises if you're underage. I'm assuming you didn't do that."

"Oh. Well, I'll ask them about it. I'll be sure you can come visit once he gets settled in."

She lifts her eyes then to look at me, and for a moment she looks so much like Mom it's like talking to a ghost. "Do you really think this is the right thing? He's our *dad*."

She always says it that way. It always feels like a knife in the gut.

"I have to."

I can't bring myself to say the rest out loud: *Someone else has to take care of him, because I can't do it anymore. Someone else has to be in charge, because it's almost impossible for me to even look at him. Someone else has to do it, because I can barely bring myself to let him out of his bedroom.*

For the first part of the drive, we sit in silence. Dad's content to lean against the door frame, head against the passenger side glass, watching the scenery pass.

Los Ojos supposedly got its name—"the eyes"—because of the way the city crouches between the mesa to the east and the river to the west. Supposedly, the craggy stone of the mesa is like the brow ridge of a face; the river cuts through like a meandering gash of a smile. The town that lies between the two is supposed to form the rest of the features, like some kind of oversized emoji writ large on the landscape.

I don't see it, personally. But if it were true, then I guess right now we're driving down the bridge of the city's nose, making our way toward the setting sun. The highway cuts through most of the town, and the outer rim of Los Ojos is a blur of tourist shops and gas stations giving way to trailer parks and run-down farms just outside city limits, adobe houses with rusted tractors and hollowed-out cars parked out front.

Then we're free of the city's grasp. The desert filling in around us, punctuated only occasionally with cattle grazing on scrub behind lines of barbed wire. Dad shifts in his seat, leaning heavily against the door but inclining his head toward me, fixing me with a hard look from one eye.

"Where are we going?"

"A doctor," I tell him, shifting my hands on the steering wheel. I make myself keep my eyes on the road. "A special kind of hospital opened up here, for people like you."

"Dead people."

"Yes. The Undead."

He falls silent for a while, as if considering this. Then, in a quieter voice, as if speaking to himself: "Don't need a doctor. Just need some goddamn peace and quiet. Just a little sleep. That's all."

I know the feeling.

I wait for Dad to speak again, to ask more questions or start to complain, but he's fallen asleep. He sleeps with his head against the window, snoring softly with each breath, and with the sunset splashing the car with violet light, he looks nearly alive. It would be easy to think that this is just another time spent picking him up from a bar, that he's just there sleeping off a night of binge drinking; it would be easy enough to think that things have gone back to how they'd once been.

But then, intermittently, he stops breathing; his body forgets to put forth the effort, and his chest falls still. And in those moments, it's impossible to ignore the fact that I'm driving down the highway with a corpse in my passenger seat. Even knowing that the world knows about the Undead, just having him in the car makes me uneasy, the way that driving with an expired license makes your nerves prickle at the sight of a cop car. Lucky for us, out here on the fringes of Los Ojos, there isn't much traffic; aside from the occasional 18-wheeler, I'm alone on the road.

This part of New Mexico is a patchwork of small towns, oil fields, and Indian reservations. The Lazarus House is set up about an hour from town, sitting right on the fringes of the reservation. We pass the casino on our way in, a brightly-lit oasis on the way to nowhere. In the gathering dark, you can see it from miles, all flashing lights and scrolling marquee. But once you pass, the highway goes dark again, a straight path with the occasional exit for a feeder road offering access to someone's sheep pasture or a dried-up oil well left over from the big natural gas boom of the last decade. There are memorials set up at some of the mile markers: crosses, teddy bears, wilting flowers, and bicycles with streamers on the handles. They lend a funereal atmosphere to the road.

I peel off an exit to take the underpass, winding my way off the beaten path and down toward the Lazarus House.

The facility itself is a converted old Spanish mission that spent a long time being—of all things—first a leper colony, then a mental institution. It lay dormant for a while, passing through the hands of a few people looking to turn the place into a historic landmark. But nobody was interested, and it was empty for a long time before the property got bought up and repurposed to house the Undead.

When I was a kid, folks used to say the place was haunted. Kids used to break in and try to play Bloody Mary. I guess it really is haunted now, in a way.

The Lazarus House is set back from the street by a long gravel drive. At the foot of this path, a gate has been set up, with a small guard station beside it. It looks more like the exit of an airport parking lot than the gate to an Undead housing facility, but then, I figure they're making up these rules as they go. There's not really a long tradition of Undead housing to draw upon.

I pull up to the gate, and a man comes out from the guard station. He's short, round, white, balding up top; a rent-a-cop sort of look to him. A fine yellow-orange dust—fake cheese from some kind of chip, I'm guessing—clings to his fingertips and works its way through the short bristles of his beard. He wipes his hand on the pants of his uniform as he approaches the car.

"You have a visitor's pass?"

"My name is Davin Montoya," I say, trying not to recoil from the heavy stench of false cheddar on his breath. "I made an intake appointment for my dad, Ignacio."

The guard leans forward, sticking his head into the cabin of the car, and looks past me to my father. Dad's still literally dead asleep, his mouth hanging slack and eyes rolled up, the whites showing through the slits of partly-open eyes. The guard, apparently satisfied with this cartoonishly macabre scene, grunts and pulls away back to his station. He wipes his hand on his pants again and punches the buttons that operate the gate.

The main building of the facility is a sprawling adobe mission, the face of it graying with age and weather. The door is tall, heavy, domed like a church door framed with stone pillars. Above the door, there's an alcove where a bell had once hung; the space is empty now, a shadowed gap like a missing tooth. Walls spread out on either side, windows barred and dark.

Beside the main building is a small, squat single-wide trailer. Unlike the mission, it's brightly lit; golden light pours out from the windows and the gap around the door. A signpost placed in front of the trailer reads "Visitor Parking," and I navigate into that space.

Dad, still sleeping, lolls bonelessly in his seat. I consider waking him and decide it would be best if I left him for now, until we're ready. I cut the engine and start to get out, hesitate. Should I crack a window for him? The question is paralyzingly absurd.

He's your dad, for fuck's sake, not a dog.

It's not like he's going to suffocate. What will it do, kill him?

I put the keys back in the ignition, turn it, and roll down a window.

The air conditioner is running full blast inside the trailer, and the door struggles against the air pressure. It slams shut behind me with a rude squelch, and the woman at the front desk looks up, an irritated expression crossing her face. Beads of sweat are prominent against her forehead despite the AC, and she's fanning herself with a sheaf of papers.

What would have been the trailer's living room has been converted into a reception area. A few scattered chairs and couches fill one area, loosely clustered around a table littered with faded magazines that look like they've been acquired third-hand. To the left: a desk, the receptionist seated behind it, her body partially obscured by the giant, ancient computer tower and monitor set up in front of her.

"Can I help you?"

"Hi. I mean, yes." I approach the desk. I'm not sure what to do with my hands; I keep slipping them into my pockets, out again, tapping my fingertips against my pants leg. "I have an intake appointment. For my dad, I mean, not for me. I'm still alive." I laugh, to cover for the nervous rambling, but it comes out weak and shrill.

Her eyes, as they fix on me, are tired and unamused. She's wearing foundation a few shades lighter than her skin tone, and I can see streaks in it down the sides of her face, tracts of sweat. She's got mascara-thick lashes and painted-on brows, with bangs curled and spiked in a way that hasn't been popular since the 90s.

"Name?"

"Montoya." I hesitate. "Davin. I mean. That's my name. My dad's name is Ignacio."

She looks up at me, then past me, then flicks her eyes back up to mine: an unspoken question.

"He's in the car," I say. "Sleeping."

Brows lift, but she says nothing. Instead, she tells me to wait a moment and presses a manicured nail onto an intercom button on her desk, calling for assistance. She doesn't look at me again, and I take that as a sign that she's done with me, so I pull back and wait.

After what feels like an eternity but is really probably just a couple of minutes, the door opens, and a shadow passes over me. I'm not sure what I was expecting to come through the doorway, but it's not this.

I'm taller than most people I know—close to 6'2"—but the guard who arrives seems to tower over me. He's built like a tank, all thick muscles and broad shoulders. There's a military air about him, something about his posture and the tidiness of his close-shaven haircut. I can't see a weapon on him, but it wouldn't surprise me to find one hidden somewhere. I also wouldn't be surprised to see him pop someone's head like a grape.

Why don't they have this guy guarding the front gate instead?

It takes me a moment to realize that he's not a security guard at all—he's an orderly. Blue scrubs. Paper shoes. A name tag that reads "Jesus," with the accent written in Sharpie over the "u."

He sees me reading his nametag and grins. "You can call me Chuy," he says, and offers a big bear-paw of a hand. I reluctantly shake it, and his grin widens. "Are you here for an intake appointment?"

"For my dad," I say, hurriedly, nervous. "Not me. I'm not dead. I mean. Obviously."

He laughs, and the warmth in it catches me off guard. His eyes sparkle when he smiles. "I figured as much. If you're a dead guy, you're in amazing shape."

I can't tell if he's hitting on me. I have no idea what to say, so I say nothing.

He keeps talking as we turn for the door. "Well, let's get started. Where's your dad?"

"In the car." I gesture toward it as we exit the trailer. I can still make out his sleeping shape, slumped against the passenger door. "Sleeping like, erm, the dead. Ha, ha."

Chuy squints to get a look at him. He doesn't laugh at my joke, but lets it hang there unacknowledged and politely ignored, like a rude noise made at an embarrassing moment. "Would you rather we left him here so you could get a look at the place first? Some people find it's easier to do the tour without their loved ones. It can be, uh, a lot to take in at once."

I nod, grateful, and follow him to the front entrance of the mission. He draws a key from a pocket of his scrubs, unlocks the heavy door, and leans into it to hold it open so I can walk through.

"This is our common area. And those, over there, are the individual rooms."

The outer wall opens, castle-like, into an open courtyard. It's weedy, empty patches of sandy ground grown through with cactus and desert grass, but there are picnic tables and chairs set out. A series of small rooms cluster around the courtyard's perimeter, rooms that at one time would have housed missionaries and, later, mental patients.

Now, every room is haunted with a living ghost.

Everywhere around me are signs of decay—the slow rot of age, the falling apart of tissue baking in the late-summer heat. It's impossible to mistake these people for being alive, and that's probably why they're herded up and kept out in the desert, away from the vulnerable eyes of the public—why this Lazarus House is set up all the way out here, why nobody's in a hurry to put Undead housing in the middle of a nice neighborhood.

It's also probably about 90% of the reason the government has all the rules in place for how and when and where the Undead can do their thing around the living. It's hard to champion for the rights of someone who can walk around with half the flesh missing from their face, especially when it'll be that way forever.

We love the dead for the same reason we love babies and pets: they're blank slates for us to project ourselves onto. It's what makes visiting a grave so cathartic. Our loved ones lie silent and inert and listen to our woes and feel about us however we need them to. They love us; they're proud of us; they watch over us, because we say they do. Visiting a grave is an exercise in wish fulfillment.

A child who never grows up lives in a perfect fantasy of potential, immortalized before they can grow to disappoint you. A dead parent loses their flaws and lives on in the memory of perfect benevolence and wisdom.

The dead returning to life fucks that all up.

Chuy steers me through the courtyard and into one wing of the building, through a hall lined on both sides with doors. "Some

37

of these rooms used to be other things," he's saying conversationally. "Prayer rooms and whatnot. We've converted pretty much all of the space into patient housing, since obviously they don't need bathrooms and dining rooms and such."

We pass down a hallway and past another row of rooms. The door to one is open. A child, barely more than a toddler, peers up at me from the door frame as I pass. He's wide-eyed, but his face has a bloated, waterlogged look; his pale skin has a tinge of purplish blue. A drowning victim; I'd put money on that. Fell into his parents' pool, maybe, or maybe he's young enough to drown in the bath. Now he's a living monument to whatever fatal mistake brought him here.

I wonder where his parents are. I wonder if they come and visit, if they still love him—or if they've washed their hands of him and walked away instead, in the spirit of closure.

I couldn't blame them. Not really.

"Sad, right?" Chuy's voice makes me jump; I'd almost forgotten he was here. "The kids do all right here, though. The older patients kind of adopt them. A lot of them had kids or grandkids of their own, you know, and this is . . . kind of a good substitute. As good as it can get, I guess."

I tear my eyes from the toddler and his solemn, waterlogged face. Chuy leads me to the end of the hall, where he starts fiddling with keys until he can unlock the door.

"Are there a lot of kids here?" I manage.

He shakes his head. "Not really. I can only think of a couple, to be honest. It's mostly older people. And the suicides." His brow furrows. "You don't see as many these days, though. I mean, since it started. People started using guns."

I flinch, remembering the man in Dad's doctor's office, the mangled meat of his missing face.

"Oh, God, sorry. I keep running my mouth. I just . . . well. Anyway. Here's where your dad will probably end up." His tone shifts, more businesslike. "As you can see, it's a nice little room. He'll have the place to himself for a while during the observation period. If he turns out to be one of the patients who does better with a roommate, we can address that later. We try to take it on kind of a case-by-case basis. Is he a really outgoing kind of guy?"

I choke on a laugh.

"Ah, well, nothing wrong with that." Chuy doesn't probe, and I don't share. I'm afraid if I say too much, they might decide to turn us away. "Anyway. Lazarus doses happen on a regular schedule, and we're really careful about monitoring that. There's doctors on staff who do all of the training. We haven't had an incident here, really, since I got hired."

"And when was that?"

"About two months now."

That doesn't exactly fill me with confidence. But thinking of Dad coming at me, the needle tearing through his skin, I don't have much room to talk.

"So, yeah. Oh! Right. Visitation. There's slots for visit dates available on our calendar. We pretty much reserve a time slot for families and hold it for you, so there's no awkwardness with visitors overlapping. You have to put in your bid a month in advance, though, if you want to change your usual day."

It would be awkward to see someone else you knew here, to meet their eyes and acknowledge that you were visiting the walking corpse of a family member. Giving your condolences to an acquaintance is already uncomfortable; trying to find words to make sense of the Undead situation is impossible.

"But if you need another day for whatever reason, just call and schedule and we'll see what we can do. I'll give you a tip. Call in the mornings—Carla works morning shift, and she's so much friendlier than Dory. You'll like her." His eyes flick downward, meeting mine, and he offers a Boy Scout smile. "But that's basically the tour. Any questions?"

I try to think, but my head's still swimming with conflicting ideas, images, anxieties. The drowned little boy and my dad's sleepily boneless body; the torn gash in his arm and the weedy courtyard. I feel like there's a lot of important things I should be asking about, but I can't think of a single one.

"It's all paid for?" I must have asked that a dozen times by now.

Chuy shrugs. "We run off government money, as far as I know. I think the reasoning is that it's easier to keep everybody in one spot than spread out all over the place. I think they're really pushing to get people to surrender their family members— I mean, have them come stay here. It's just easier on everyone, is all. But yeah. Should be pretty much free for you. Actually, you might make a couple bucks on it, if your dad's drawing disability."

That idea brings another twisted, sad little half-smile to my face. His disability check is the most money Dad's given to the household since I was a teenager.

CHAPTER FOUR

CHUY FOLLOWS ME back to the car. By the time we get there, Dad's awake, sitting upright in the passenger seat and hugging his knees to his chest. He looks sullen, withdrawn, but he doesn't put up much fight when Chuy goes to that side of the car and coaxes him out. I watch them from a distance, keeping the car between us as if sheltering myself from becoming involved.

He's good with him, I think, watching them. *Dad will be so much better off here.*

I try to tell myself that's why I feel so much relief, like a weight uncoiling from my chest. I try to tell myself I'm just happy that my dad's getting the kind of care he needs.

I don't linger too long or make any big goodbyes. I figure it'll just make things harder on him, cause a scene. I'll play it cool, give him some time to get settled, and then come back to explain my decision once he's had a chance to try it. If he hates it, I'll take him home; no harm done.

I cast a final, grateful look in Chuy's direction as the orderly guides my dad inside and to his new chamber. Then I'm back in the trailer, signing paperwork and trying not to let my eyes glaze over as I initial release after release. The words on the contracts all blur together, and by the time I'm finally ready to go, it's dark outside. Clouds obscure the stars, bringing the sky down closer to the earth like a low ceiling.

I pause in the car, watching as rain begins to fall—occasional fat rain drops that turn slowly into heavy spatters that splash across the windshield—and punch in Zoe's number on my cell phone. I wait; nothing. Straight to voice mail.

"Hey, Zoe. It's me. Look, I know you're probably still upset with me. Just wanted to let you know it's done. I think this is for the best. We can talk about it tonight, though. I'm heading home and we can grab a pizza and hash it all out. See you in an hour or so."

In New Mexico, rain always takes you by surprise. Storms are sudden. Clouds form and burst within moments, flash-flooding the low-lying streets and filling the arroyos. Then they're gone just as soon as they arrived, leaving water evaporating from streets under the oppressive heat, moisture wicked back into a thirsty earth. Within an hour of a big storm, there's usually no sign that anything even happened.

But during those brief moments when the storm is raging, for just a little while it seems like the world might end. It doesn't matter how many times you've seen it happen; every time the skies open up, it's easy to think that the rain won't stop until everything has been washed away.

There's no traffic on the drive home. I roll down the empty highway and marvel at the black-gray sky: ominous clouds that gathered in the space of an hour to blot out the setting sun. Rain spatters the windows, slowly gaining in speed and volume. Overhead, lightning flickers through the clouds, the only light in the complete darkness of this old state highway. The sun should be low and thick on the horizon, but it's almost dark enough with the cloud cover to pass for night.

I'm trying hard to keep my thoughts on the moment, to keep them from straying back toward Dad and his fellow living ghosts haunting the Lazarus House, but the isolation isn't making it easy. Out here in the darkness, it's like there's no world but what's inside the car. Only the semicircle of light granted by the headlights, and a thick curtain of rain beyond the nose of the car. Each mile is driven on faith that the road continues past the edge of the light, that the world out there still exists.

The drive home seems to last an eternity. With rain sheeting down, obscuring my vision, I'm forced to drive below the speed limit. Time itself seems to slow and distort, like what's supposed to happen at the edge of a black hole; it's as if the further I get from the Lazarus House, the thicker the air becomes, like its gravitational pull is holding me in place.

I pass an abandoned car, occasionally, pulled over on the shoulder: vehicles that broke down, or cars that were stolen and dumped, or the part-time homes of people with nowhere else to go. Otherwise, the road is quiet and empty. I turn on the radio for company, to drown out the silence and the loneliness and that uneasy feeling that's begun crawling down my spine.

" —healthcare disaster. There's no reason we should be paying for these people. They can work for their own keep."

"You're suggesting that their condition isn't a disability?"

"I'm suggesting that we have a population who don't feel any pain, who don't need to eat or sleep, and instead of putting them to work we're letting them—pardon the expression—we're letting them rot in nursing homes and keeping them around with the money of our honest taxpayers . . . "

I quickly switch the radio to another station, classic rock cut through with the crackle of static.

When people first began to come back from the dead, there was a flurry of spiritual interest in them. What had they seen? What was it like? Did they talk to God? Did they see the light?

The dead, by and large, never seemed to have satisfying answers. Everyone's stories were different.

There was one guy who wrote a book about it. He called it *The Death Experience*, and it was on the bestseller list for a while. He went on tour, signed a bunch of copies, talked on the early morning shows. He had all sorts of stories about what he'd seen: how he'd glimpsed Hell itself, seen the fiery pits crawling with demons.

According to his book, he'd sat outside the very gates of the underworld and heard the anguished screams of the people inside. And, supposedly, he was sent back to tell everyone left standing to repent their sins, right their wrongs, change their ways and avoid that terrible fate.

He made some good money off of it, I guess. But it didn't last too long; just another flash in the pan, swept away and forgotten by the next big thing. He never wrote another book. Maybe he's sitting in a facility somewhere, like my dad. Maybe he went off his meds and went on a murder spree. Maybe he decided that the fires of hell weren't so bad after all and decided to give the death thing another try. Who knows?

Anyway, his story didn't get much traction after those first few months, because nobody else seemed to come forward with a story that was the same, at least not one that proved to be authentic. A few of the people who came forward claiming to have seen the same hell hadn't even really died—they'd just been clinically dead, brought back as a living person by the powers of modern medicine, not as a walking corpse, the genuine article. One of them hadn't even died at all; he was just in it for a few seconds of fame or notoriety.

Other people's stories, the ones that seemed legit, were all over the place.

Some people claimed to have met God, describing him in turns as an old man, a woman, a pulsing ball of light, a winged creature, something that defied explanation. Others claimed to have seen their long-departed family members. Some supposedly saw glimpses into the future, or the past, or rose up and saw their bodies beneath them. Some people saw nothing at all.

Eventually, the curiosity wore down. People stopped caring so much about the stories. There was nothing new in them; no insight, no spiritual answers to prove or deny much of anything.

Some people still aren't even sure if the Undead are, in any real sense, actually dead.

What is death?

What does it mean to die?

44

No one knows, and they certainly aren't asking the people who've been there anymore. No one is interested in the answers.

Half an hour in, the wind starts to pick up. Lightning shreds the clouds overhead, thunder rumbling, the wind buffeting the car on roads growing increasingly slick with moisture.

The radio station has tipped the scales from music to static, words just occasionally peeking through like some sort of transmission from a different world. I shut it off to silence the crackling and buzzing, and a terrible silence settles into the car. The flesh on the back of my neck prickles, that unnerved feeling like someone's watching you, and I realize that my hands hurt from gripping the steering wheel too hard. I take a deep breath, exhaling slowly, easing up the tension in my hands and shoulders.

There's no reason to be this edgy. It's just a storm.

The windshield wipers squeal against the glass, but rain obscures my vision too quickly for me to turn them to a lower speed. Outside of the circle of my headlights, the world is a blanket of darkness. Up ahead, the highway narrows over a bridge; a guard rail is missing. I can't read the sign, but I know it reads *Rio de Animas.*

River of Souls.

When I was little, my grandmother told me a story of how the river got its name. My grandmother was full of stories. She'd pull me onto her knee and tell them to me in the evening, even when I was getting too big to sit there. We spent a lot of time at Grandma's house, and for a while—when I was ten or so—we lived there while Mom dealt with doctors and medical issues and the question of whether or not the cancer had returned.

Grandma's stories weren't always pleasant.

My mother's mother, she'd married a Sephardic Jew and

raised her children to be Jewish, but she believed in something else—something old, primal, superstitious. And so she told me stories about La Llorona and skinwalkers and El Chupacabra. She told me about ghost sickness and El Cucuy and *espiritus malos*. They were stories to frighten and entertain, stories to keep you from playing in arroyos or venturing out in the dark, but there was never a moment that I doubted that she believed every word of them.

My grandmother's story about Rio de Animas is a La Llorona story. The way she told it, a woman had two children—a boy and a girl, just like me and Zoe. They were illegitimate, born to a man who had promised to marry her; but he went back on his promise, marrying a woman of wealth and standing instead. A fallen woman—unable to care for her young children, desperately angry at the man who had scorned her—she clutched her children to her breast and waded into the water, letting the current sweep them all to their deaths.

But while her children passed on into another life, Grandma would tell me in a hushed tone, the woman's soul was caught in the river. She haunted the banks, eternally searching for children to replace those she had lost, children to keep her company in eternity.

According to Grandma, a lot of kids died in that river, pulled down into its dark and muddy depths. And in the summer, when monsoon season would swell the banks with flash floods, when kids caught playing too close would inevitably drown in its waters, we'd watch it on the news and Grandma would cast me a knowing look and I would *know*, the kind of knowing that happens in the pit of your stomach, that it was La Llorona.

Now, driving over the bridge, rain sheeting down the windshield, I can't help but think about those kids, the ghosts of the river.

If dead people can come back to life, I think, *why can't the river be filled with ghosts?*

The glare of my headlights settles on something up ahead, in the center of the road. It was invisible seconds before, fading into the shadows of night, but now it's in the spotlight; and although a fraction of a second passes, the image burns perfectly into my mind.

It's a humanoid figure, dressed in tattered clothes. The true colors are washed out by darkness and the glare of headlights, leaving everything in a blurry gray, but the shape is identifiable—the slender torso, the long arms, the fold of its knees. It sits crouched in the middle of the highway, half bent over something bulky in the road. A deer, maybe, or a sheep. Maybe a large dog.

Whatever it is, the figure in the highway is eating it. When my headlights hit it, the figure looks up, twin circles of wide eyes reflecting white-green in the glare, and a messy chunk of meat spills over its chin and dribbles down its front. Its long white fingers are buried in soft flesh and fur.

The wheel jerks in my hand, as though acting on its own. I pump the brake, and the brakes respond with a thump and grind. The car lurches to the right, and the tires lose their grip on the damp concrete. The tail end of the car, fed by inertia, swings around, and suddenly the car is spinning. I'm pinned to the door by centrifugal force, the wheel ripped from my hands, and then a tire snags the edge of the bridge, slipping through the gap left by the broken guard rail, and I'm staring down perpendicular at the river, fat and dark with rain.

A feeling of weightlessness as the car tips forward, its nose hanging over the side of the bridge. I'm thrown back against my seat and then slammed forward, the sudden impact with the ground below thrusting me against the steering column. Something crunches.

The airbag, late to the party, explodes against my face. Shattered glass blows back with it. There's a terrible pain in my gut, an awful swelling explosion of agony.

And then there's nothing at all.

CHAPTER FÍVE

THEY SAY THAT when you die, your life flashes before your eyes.

A group of scientists studied it once, to see if it was anything more than a cliché. They wired electrodes up to a bunch of rats, monitoring their brains, and pumped them full of euthanasia solution. Sure enough: brain activity spikes in the seconds after the rest of the body's systems have failed. A final dying gasp for the electrical current in the mind, synapses firing to stitch together memories and emotions into a final dream.

Maybe death, then, is the same as sleep.

I wonder what the rats dreamed about, as their bodies failed?

Time means nothing. It could be seconds, or hours, or days; there's no point of reference. Everything is darkness. Emptiness, and my awareness of that emptiness: consciousness surrounded by nothing.

Then, at the corners of my vision, crackles of light—as if something were chewing at the edges of a dark blanket. Rats, again. It always comes back to rats, somehow.

Rats dreaming.

The rats in the walls.

The light flickers and expands, sending out spider webs of cracks that cut through the blackness. I try to blink, grimacing against the brightness, but I have no eyelids. Open or closed, my eyes see the same thing.

I am my consciousness, and the darkness is in my head.
Am I dreaming?

That's the question I wonder as the world around me brightens and I become aware of a nonsensical stream of images. It's like watching the odds and ends from a film reel that's been edited together—like someone taped together all the bits that ended up on the cutting room floor.

Mom, healthy, whole. Her short, plump body and frizzy hair, so much like Zoe's; the easy smile that was always ready to appear, like a peek at sunshine behind clouds.

The blue-gray light of a hospital corridor, fluorescent bulbs humming and flickering overhead. Zoe asleep beside me, her head on my shoulder. The game on my phone, its sound effects the only noise in the deserted lobby. We were too young to be there; the front desk tried to send us home, because it was too late for children to be visiting. But there was nowhere else for us to go, not with our grandmother in the grave and her daughter soon to follow.

Dad's body lying insensate on the couch, his mouth lolling open, his eyes glassy and staring at nothing. A fly buzzing around his face, crawling over ashy skin, the way it rubbed its legs together as if preparing to feast on the froth of vomit at the corner of his mouth.

Dad, alive. Dressed in his military uniform, dress whites, attending the funeral of a friend. Me, just a kid, hugging close to his leg, fingers curled around the fabric of his slacks. The crack of gunfire, shots fired in the sky. Rain coming down, as if invited by the artificial thunder, as if the bullets had cracked open the heavens to leak tears over the mourners.

Other images aren't so poignant.

The flutter of a receipt, swirling in the wind. The red glow of tail lights in traffic. A smear of chocolate frosting on a blue plate. The pattern of mountains and valleys in peeling drywall.

Random shapes, geometric angles and irregular blobs, in an array of colors. They dance over my vision, as if my brain were trying to reconstruct reality from its component parts. As if the world were a sweater that had been unraveled, all of the threads now twisting and gaining new significance, forming into different shapes.

At the edge of my vision: half-realized creatures, monsters from nightmares I had as a child, images mostly forgotten from films and video games. It's a confusing mess, and I watch with the awareness that none of this is real—or maybe all of it is.

I don't know how long I dream. All I know is that, eventually, the images recede again, and I'm returned to nothing, darkness, emptiness.

My senses return to me slowly.

Smells: motor oil. Gasoline. The taste of blood, salty-sweet and metallic. The sulfurous stench of mud, dirty rainwater, the bacterial funk of standing water. The sound of faraway traffic, of nearby birds. Then, finally, vision. Darkness, greyness, blurriness. Sight.

I'm lying facedown in the mud. I struggle to lift my head, blinking away the film from my eyes and trying to get my bearings. My arms and legs move, uncoordinated, sliding in the muck, before they're able to push me up. I crouch there on all fours and wait for the dizziness to fade, the ringing in my ears to abate.

Feeling is the last thing to return. For a few blissful moments, I'm totally numb.

And then the pain comes, sweeping across me like fire, and the intensity sends me back into the mud. I lie there, paralyzed by it, unable to comprehend. My muscles are burning. A deep ache settles into my bones, that rotten feeling of a tooth with a dying root. And something inside feels . . . wrong. Sluggish. Still.

It's the feeling of my heart not beating.

It's the feeling of my lungs not breathing.

The panic is peripheral, distant, as if felt in another body. I struggle to my knees and force a deep breath, sucking down air hungrily. That's a mistake. The pain in my lungs is terrible, searing, and they clench in my chest and shudder through my torso. It twists, then makes a return trip, bringing up the contents of my stomach and . . . something else.

Until today, "puking my guts out" was just an expression.

But now I'm watching helplessly as my gut spasms and I'm vomiting up bloody chunks of . . . *something* . . . from deep inside. Gobbets of meat wrench free from my innards and pool into the damp mud. It looks like carne adovada, and that idea makes me vomit again, dredging up more blood, more chunks of flesh, until my throat is raw and my guts are shredded.

It stops, finally. I fall back on my heels and scramble away from the gore. My body is trembling, but I feel—strangely—a little better. Like something has been purged.

But I don't risk taking another breath. I don't risk thinking about what it means that my heart is quiet behind the ruined cage of my ribs.

It's only then that I remember about the car. The bridge. The rain.

Overhead, the sun is out. It's late morning. I've been out here all night.

I'm on the banks of the Rio de Animas, surrounded by detritus. The river should be brown and swollen with rainwater, but it's barely a trickle here, probably dried up with time. How long have I been out? The car is a long way off. How did I get here? Did I get thrown? Did I crawl out somehow? Get washed downstream?

Conjecture is impossible. I remember nothing after impact. Just the dreams after, and those are fading.

What I know: I've been out here all night. Maybe longer. Maybe it's been days.

Zoe is alone.

I have to get home.

It's a long climb back up to the highway, and with every movement I'm half afraid that the effort will wrench my limbs free of their sockets. I imagine leaving pieces of myself behind, body parts working themselves loose until I'm reduced to fragments of meat. But it doesn't happen, and I pull myself up onto the road and lie for a long time on the shoulder and try to come up with a plan.

I'm a long ways from anywhere. It's all desert out here, windswept rocks painted the colors of sunsets, and scrubby brush that dots the horizon. If I had a car, I'd be maybe half an hour from home. Maybe closer to the casino. I could go inside and ask for help.

But I don't have a usable car. I'm not even sure I have usable legs.

For the hundredth time, I shove my hands into my pockets, looking for my phone. It's long gone. It fell out somewhere—in the car, in the river. It doesn't matter now; it's not coming back.

I wonder how worried Zoe might be, and that more than anything is what's driving me forward. It's just easier not to think about the rest; it's easier to ignore my mangled body and what this shit means for my future. The worry buzzing on repeat through my skull is all about Zoe.

She's lost everything already. Mom. Dad. Not me. Not today, if I can help it.

So I heave myself back onto my feet and start walking, because at least that feels like doing something. I don't know where I'm going (West? The sun seems to be creeping in that direction.), and I don't know what I'll do when I get there, but at least as long as I'm walking I'm not thinking about everything that's happened.

A truck passes, and the rush of wind shoves me sideways; I sway unsteadily and nearly fall, but the truck is hurtling away without slowing. No one's going to stop for me, I think. No one's going to pick up a hitchhiker, not out here. If I'm lucky, they'll assume that I'm a drunk, and they'll leave me staggering here on the side of the road to walk it off and find my way home.

If I'm not so lucky . . . well.

I remember the photograph on Zoe's monitor, the Undead with his brains splattered across the asphalt. I try, hard, to think about something else.

The pain in my body has transformed from a dull ache into a distant sensation, like the numb realization of feelings lurking beneath a morphine drip—the knowledge that, somewhere, your body is damaged irreparably, but you can't feel it directly. I keep walking. I can't think of anything else to do.

I become aware of the car before my senses catch up; that peripheral awareness, the sense that allows you to know that someone has entered a room or is watching over your shoulder. Then, the sound: the crunch of gravel beneath tires, the quiet hum of an engine. The scent of exhaust, and that peculiar under-odor of hot metal.

I freeze, like a rabbit caught in headlights, and wait. The car doesn't pass. It slows and comes to a stop beside me, motor humming. I turn, slowly, to look.

The car that rolls up is a cherry-red Mercedes Benz. It's a newer model, but it already shows signs of wear: dust settling into the grooves, flecks of paint missing from around the wheel wells, small dents freckling the edges of the doors.

A dark-tinted passenger side window rolls down, and a small plume of smoke exits, curling out the window and up into the sky. There's only one person in the car, and the driver leans toward the passenger window.

"You need a ride?"

CHAPTER SIX

"**Y**OU NEED A RIDE?"
The speaker is a white guy; maybe my age, maybe a little older. He's pale, with dark eyes and a shock of bright pink hair. There's something about his eyes that catches my attention, some depth that suggests the kind of still waters that will pull you under, drown you. They form a weird contrast to his skin, to the bubblegum-shaded spikes of hair. He's out of place out here, even more incongruous than his flashy-but-battered car.

He leans over the passenger seat, head dipping below the line of the window frame, and opens the door; it swings wide, inviting. I stare, first at the open door, then up at him, uncomprehending.

I look like shit. I'm muddy, with blood and vomit staining my torn clothes. I'm covered in bruises. I'm in Middle of Nowhere, New Mexico. And here's some rich kid in a Mercedes offering me a ride, no questions asked. I'm not sure if I should be grateful or afraid.

What's he going to do, kill me?

The beginning of a hysterical laugh catches in my throat, and my lungs protest at its attempts to escape. Laughing needs air, and I know all too well what happened the last time I sucked down a big gulp of the stuff.

"Hey, buddy," the pink-haired guy says. There's a hint of accent in his words, the slow drawl of the Deep South, but it's muted, as if he were trying to cover it. "You okay?"

The incredulous look I shoot him speaks volumes.

He laughs. "Okay, I get it. But come on. Just get in the car before somebody a whole hell of a lot less friendly than me comes along. This isn't the stretch of highway you want to be caught dead on, if you know what I mean."

I blink at him. Overhead, clouds shift, and the sun beats down; it burns against my skin, but the feeling is distant, like my body belongs to somebody else.

But the door stays open, and I climb inside, folding my long legs into the sports car. I struggle to find the mechanism to move the seat back. I buckle my seat belt, and the absurdity of it nearly tears another ill-considered laugh from my throat.

The driver's eyes stay on me, watching; a brow lifts when I turn to face him. "Safety first," he remarks, dryly, as I buckle.

He isn't wearing his seat belt.

"I'm Randy," he says by way of introduction. "An' you look like you've been having quite a day."

There's no way to respond to that, so I don't say anything. I'm still trying pretty hard not to think about what happened. If I don't think about it, I don't have to deal with it, and I don't have the energy to deal with it.

He looks at me expectantly, making no move to put the car in gear. We stay parked on the side of the road, the gravel shoulder a few feet from the bridge, and he takes a long drag from the cigarette he's been holding between two fingers of his left hand.

I take a deep, painful breath. Smoke stings the inside of my nose. My lungs ache, the knife-point stabbing pain of congestion, but I don't throw up again. Maybe there's nothing left in there to puke up. Maybe my body's reluctantly accepted its fate.

"Davin," I rasp, finally, in a voice like sandpaper over stone.

"Well, Davin," he says, dropping his hand to the gearshift, "you got somewhere you need to be?"

"Los Ojos," I say. The sibilants wheeze out of me, lingering in the air like a hiss, the way you'd expect a ghost to talk. My fingertips, without my realizing, reach for my pocket; my hand pats the front of my jeans, searching for a phone that isn't there.

Randy's eyes follow the motion, but he says nothing. Instead he nods. "You've got a ways to go still," he points out, and navigates the Mercedes off the shoulder and back toward the road. "You're a long way from anything."

So are you, I want to say, but I don't want to waste the effort. Breathing, right now, is something I want to avoid as much as possible; I don't want to expend unnecessary energy making small talk.

"Anyway, lucky for you, that's jus' where I'm heading," he says, and I'm thrust back in my seat as the car guns forward, accelerating swiftly to catch up with highway speeds.

I flinch at the acceleration, memories bursting into my head like stars: the crunch of metal, the crash of glass, the feeling of my body sailing through space. A quiet sound escapes my lips, coming from somewhere deep in my chest.

"Car accident?" Randy asks mildly. He doesn't wait for me to reply. "It's generally considered rude to ask how somebody died, but we all find out in the end anyway. So I'm just going to make my guess now—car accident."

"How . . . did you . . . ?"

He inclines his head toward me, brows lifted, lips curled into a wry twist of a smile. "Know that you were dead? Davin, buddy, I hate to tell you this, but you couldn't look more like a fresh corpse if somebody dressed you up in a suit and laid you out on a satin pillow."

Something in my face must have changed, because his expression darkens. He turns his eyes back to the road, a muscle setting in his jaw, eyes narrowing by a fraction. It's a moment before he speaks again.

"Was that insensitive? Sorry. I'm not used to conversation with Breathers. Or, ah, recently-non-Breathers."

"Breathers?"

"Breathers." He lifts a hand to gesture vaguely; the car drifts toward the other lane, and I flinch. "People who are still alive. It's what we call them. It's a fuckin' stupid name though, if you ask me, because breathing is one of those things we can still do. For the most part."

"Oh. So you're—"

"Dead as a doornail, yep."

"So how did you . . . ?"

"Die?" He doesn't take his eyes from the road this time. "Didn't I just tell you? It's a rude question to ask."

He says nothing else; I wait for a laugh and an explanation, but none comes. The silence doesn't bother me. Talking hurts too much right now anyway, and I don't know what to say. I'm in over my head, and I can't make sense of my jumbled-up thoughts. Everything feels funny, like waking up expecting a hangover but realizing you're still drunk.

I wedge myself against the door and try to get a better look at him. He's small-statured, probably barely taller than Zoe, but he carries himself in a way that makes him seem bigger. The shock of his pink hair is bold against his skin, and seems to lend it some color. He's not just white; he's milky, vaguely translucent, with a bluish hint.

He wears the sports car as comfortably as his designer clothes, and I can't imagine what he could be doing in Los Ojos. Maybe he's some artist type passing through on the way to Santa Fe, I think, some foreign transplant who hasn't yet figured out how much he stands out.

Beyond the fold of his collar, I can barely make out traces of faded purple, a bruise standing out against the skin, like that left by a rope tightened around his throat.

We drive in silence for a while, desert landscape flashing by: stony hills worn to smooth curves by the wind, sagebrush and yucca standing against the horizon, sheep grazing behind barbed wire. Burnt-out shells of homes, old adobe alongside crumbling aluminum single-wide trailers. Billboards that read things like: *Indian Trading Post—Authentic Pottery and Jewelry* and *It's . . . THE THING!!!* beckon us to pull off at upcoming exits.

"So what's your story?" Randy asks, picking up the thread of conversation as if there hadn't been a long gap of awkward silence, as if the last several miles hadn't been punctuated by the rattling wheeze of my dead lungs. "Had a few too many drinks at the casino? Traveling out to get hammered at a bonfire out in the desert?"

"Not drunk," I rasp out, offended.

"My bad, my bad. Somebody hit you then?"

"Drove off the bridge." If asking how somebody died is rude, he's being kind of an asshole. But I guess it's his right to know what he's dealing with, since I'm currently plastering his car in mud and guck. "Lost control in the rain."

"Ah, sure. Damn New Mexicans don't know a goddamn thing about driving in the rain." He glances at me, a smile quirking the corner of his mouth. When I don't smile back at his ribbing, he shifts topics. "You weren't getting plastered then. So what brings you to the middle of fuckin' nowhere?"

"The Lazarus House. My dad." I want to explain more, but I'm taken over by a coughing fit that threatens to splatter over the dashboard of his nice car. I bury my face in the crook of an elbow and am useless for a while, heaving and gagging.

"There's probably some napkins in the glove box." He reaches across me to unhinge it, leaning partway into my lap. The glove box falls open, showing a cluttered mix: brown paper napkins, a pristine Mercedes service manual, a very battered map of New Mexico, an optimistically large number of condoms.

I grab a fistful of napkins and cough into them, and the car falls silent again for a while as the sports car chews up miles and my insides recover from trying to escape.

Randy doesn't ask where I live, and I shift uneasily in my seat as the mile markers count down. The exit to Los Ojos looms to the right, but the car glides smoothly past without decelerating. A small, choked noise catches in my throat.

He glances at me, a momentary sidelong shift of the eyes, and grins. "Don't worry. I'll get you home. But I have to take care of something first—and besides, you need some cleaning up. You look like you spent the night in a grave, no offense."

"Have you . . . " I stop, clear my throat, try to swallow back the pain. "Got a phone?"

"Sure," he says casually, without asking for any further clarification—a *mi casa es tu casa* gesture. He wriggles in his seat, pulling an iPhone from a hip pocket. He slides his thumb over the touchscreen, not looking down, and unlocks it. The Mercedes swerves slightly with his maneuvering, but he corrects its path and hands the phone over without looking at me. It's one of the newer models, but the case is chipped and the top corner of the screen is badly cracked. Like his car, it has the appearance of something both expensive and neglected.

I take it and stare at it a long moment, realizing with dawning horror that I don't remember Zoe's number. Who the fuck memorizes phone numbers anymore?

Maybe I can message her on Facebook or something, I think, rapidly pulling up the browser. Nothing; no response. I should know better than to expect an internet connection out here.

"No luck?"

I shake my head mutely and set his phone down in the center console. I notice that there's a bloody thumbprint on the screen that wasn't there before and it actually hits me, for the first time, what a mess I must be making of his car.

It gives me a sudden rush of gratitude toward this stranger, this man who doesn't mind a walking corpse leaving blood and God knows what else all over the interior of his sports car.

But the gratitude is followed quickly by suspicion. Who would do this? Who picks up hitchhikers in the desert?

Lonely people. And people with ulterior motives.

The desert slowly gives way to scattered buildings. Randy takes an exit, pulling from the interstate onto another highway—an older one, run down with age. The low-slung car rattles against the rough asphalt, and I feel a twisting in my gut that might be car sickness or might be more chunks of innards working their way out. Either way, I swallow it back and stare resolutely forward, willing myself to be calm.

We're on the outskirts of Los Ojos, unincorporated county property that rests outside the city limits. I catch flickering glimpses of buildings as they pass by. A gas station. A mom-and-pop pizzeria. A boarded-up pool hall. Randy turns onto a side street, then another. We pass a church, its whitewashed sides peeling, and then a mobile home park. This he pulls into, drawing into the gravel parking lot before an old single-wide trailer.

It's green and faded, the aluminum siding stained in a wide wedge from the constant drip of a swamp cooler. The door hangs awkwardly on its hinges; light from inside leaks through the gaps. But the yard is tidy, the gravel free of debris. There are potted plants outside, strawberries and tomatoes sitting in terracotta homes. Laundry hangs on a line between the corner of the roof and the edge of the chain-link fence surrounding the space. It reminds me of my grandmother's house, that place where I spent so much of my childhood, and in a way it's comforting.

I know too, immediately, that this is not Randy's house. Not just because of the incongruity of a Mercedes in a trailer park, but because these settings tell stories of opposing personalities. Randy's belongings are all expensive and neglected; whoever owns this trailer has tended to it with care, even if it's worthless from age.

I climb out of the car. My legs, unfolding, fail to hold my weight. They give way beneath me like limbs that have fallen asleep. I sway on my feet, clutching at the door as my knees give out; my vision swims, threatening to vanish entirely as it darkens around the edges. An insistent ringing starts in my ears, a high-pitched whine that dampens all other sound.

I blink rapidly, trying to clear my vision, trying to regain feeling in my limbs. Something in my chest strains against my ribs.

"You good?" It takes me a moment to place the voice, to bring my consciousness back to the here-and-now, but it starts to come back to me and I nod.

Randy swims back into my vision, seemingly distant though he's barely a foot away, a hand cupping my upper arm to steady me.

"It's your heart," he explains. "It still beats, sometimes. It's part of what keeps this whole dog-and-pony show running. But it gets confused or something; stops workin' sometimes, goes into overdrive other times."

"Do—do you get used to it?"

"Not really."

His hand withdraws from my arm. I can still feel his grip, the ghost of an imprint left by strong fingertips. My skin feels like memory foam, slow to refill after the pressure's gone. He turns for the gate, makes his way through and toward the trailer's crooked door. I stumble after, afraid of falling.

The door opens before Randy has a chance to knock.

"Thought I heard somebody pull up."

The man in the doorway isn't much older than my dad. He's white, but permanently tanned and leathery, with the look of someone accustomed to long hours of hard labor outdoors. I can't quite tell what color his hair is; it might be blond or gray. It seems nearly colorless, as though someone has turned down the saturation. His eyes, somewhere between blue and gray-green, have that same desaturated look. He seems faded, like an old photograph—a memory—a ghost.

"You brought a guest." He shifts his colorless eyes to look me over, taking in the details of my torn clothing, the blood, the caved-in angle of my torso. "Looks like you've had quite a night, son."

I attempt a smile. My vision flickers at the edges, like burns in celluloid.

"John Ashley," the man says, extending a hand as though there were nothing at all strange about shaking the hand of a corpse who's standing on your doorstep. "But everybody calls me Ash."

"Davin." I take his hand. It's cool to the touch, dry but firm, like a leather glove stuffed with pebbles.

He withdraws his hand and I sway again; Randy's hand catches me in the small of the back, preventing me from toppling backward down the trailer's rickety steps.

"I think we can catch up with the small talk inside."

"Ah. Yes." Ash withdraws into the doorway, allowing us passage, and I walk inside with a gentle prod from Randy.

Inside, the trailer is just as old and worn-down as it seemed from outside. The interior is dated, shades of avocado and orange furniture nestled against peeling faux-wood laminate walls. But it's kept immaculately clean, and it has the feel of a space that's been well-loved.

"Mind if we borrow your bathroom?" Randy asks. His hand is still in the small of my back; I lean into it, because the physical sensation gives me something to anchor myself to while the world threatens to spin out of control around me.

"I'll get you some towels," Ash says without hesitation. "I might have some spare clothes that could fit, too. I'll take a look."

He disappears down the hallway, and I stand awkwardly before Randy gives me a nudge. "Second door on the left," he says. "I'll be around if you need anything."

I nod and head inside.

The bathroom is small, with peeling green Formica counters patterned like marble. The linoleum under my feet is warped and stained. Beneath that, the floor feels hollow, and I move gingerly, aware of every creak, afraid the old floor might give way entirely.

I start to peel off my clothes, grimacing as they stick, the blood gluing them against my body. It feels the way I imagine a full-body wax might feel, except it's not just hair that comes loose. The flesh of my torso peels free too, like the blistered skin of a roasted green chile, and I barely manage to bite back the scream.

But the pain is nothing compared to the general ache overtaking my body.

All this time, the media and the experts and everyone else have been clear on the point that Undead don't feel pain. The nerve endings don't work properly, they say. The Undead may look gruesome, with their impossible-to-heal wounds, but they aren't really hurting anymore.

I believed that. I comforted myself with that each night as I locked Dad up in his bedroom-shaped prison cell. And now, firsthand, I've learned in the worst way possible that the entire thing is bullshit. Because I hurt more now than I've ever hurt in my life, and the deep ache that settles into my body is so all-consuming that it must be here to stay. The pain has become part of me. It's been less than 24 hours, maybe, and already I'm forgetting what it felt like to be without pain.

I drop my muddy, bloodstained clothes to the floor and take a few tentative, shuddering steps to the tub. Climbing over the lip is torture; I balance precariously on one leg, moving sluggishly and apprehensively to pull myself up and in. I'm sure that at any moment I'll fall, but I stay upright, and manage to get the curtain drawn and the water turned on.

Old pipes groan in protest. The water comes in sputters at first, pressure building, before the stream grows consistent. The water takes a while to warm up, and I stand under the cool spray, grimacing at every knife-point drop as it explodes against my ruined flesh. It hurts, but it's an exquisite sort of pain; it feels the way you'd imagine a baptism by fire might feel, as if a part of you were systematically stripped and burned away to leave you raw and clean and pure.

My vision darkens at the edges again, and before I can brace myself I'm falling, my legs crumpling, my feet slipping against the faux-porcelain of the tub. I lose my orientation in space; I can't tell if I'm upright or lying flat. I can't tell if the jolts of pain are fresh or old. Everything is distant, as though connected to some other body, in some other time, some other place.

Then there's nothing. Darkness. Loss of sensation. Time stretches and warps like taffy.

Then the feeling of hands, fingertips against my skin, the firm touch of someone grasping my upper arms and tugging me upright. The water stops. My head lolls, half-conscious, and I think: *Am I finally dying?*

It's an oddly comforting thought.

CHAPTER SEVEN

MAYBE I DIDN'T *die in that car accident. Maybe everything has been a terrible misunderstanding. Maybe I was just badly injured, bleeding internally, and it's finally caught up with me. Maybe it's all over.*

A sharp pain, a needle stabbing through flesh.

Warmth spreads through me like the burn of liquor. I feel it moving under my skin and deep in my veins, inch by inch, pushing the sludge of a corpse's blood. It moves through my extremities and into my core, where something in my chest shudders and heaves.

In the darkness, I'm hyper-aware of my body, of every sensation. Air fills my lungs, flooding the millions of tiny pockets in the tissue like re-inflated bubble wrap, and I feel every single one of them. I feel the blood moving beneath my skin, the constant rush through veins, the persistent pulse of arteries, the blushing creep of capillaries. I feel the tiny electrical impulses that branch from my brain down my spine, across the millions of nerve endings.

I have never felt so alive.

My vision clears, darkness breaking apart into black islands—first rimmed in light, then drifting apart, until only a few stray specks cloud my line of sight.

The trembling in my extremities, the weakness, is gone. My legs no longer feel dead and numb; feeling returns to them in pinpricks, tiny explosions like the bursting bubbles of a sparkling wine.

I feel . . . fine.

Nothing hurts. Not even the still-open wounds, the bruises and abrasions scattered over my body, the places where skin peeled off with my clothes or burst on impact in the car. Not even the jagged edges of whatever's torn loose deep down in my gut.

I blink a few more times, clearing and focusing my vision, and my eyes meet a pair of dark brown ones, hung upside down in a pale face.

It takes a moment to make sense of what I'm seeing. I re-orient myself in space, letting my brain catch up with my overloaded senses.

I'm lying in the tub, legs folded awkwardly beneath me where they crumpled. Randy is kneeling on the floor beside me, one arm wrapped around my body, hand under an armpit, holding me up. His other hand, rested on the edge of the tub, holds a needle near my outstretched arm. His face is inches from mine, and the look in his eyes is more amusement than concern.

"What—"

Randy half-smiles with one corner of his mouth. "You should have showered sitting down."

It occurs to me, belatedly, that I'm naked. I shift slightly, in a feeble and far-too-late attempt to cover up, and the smirk glimmers in Randy's eyes.

"I won't say I hate the view," he says. "But that's really not what I came in here for."

He pulls away, drawing his arm from beneath my shoulders, and reaches for the towel, which he hands me. I lay it over my lap, still feeling too disoriented to move from my position.

"You drugged me."

"I did, a bit." His eyes meet mine, impassive, a gentle challenge. "You feel better?"

"What did you give me?" I struggle to pull myself up, scrabbling against the tub for a better grip, trying to find my feet. My toes make swirls in the blood smeared over the fake porcelain.

Randy stands, extending a hand to help me. "Lazarus," he

says, in response to my question. "It's been all over the news. I'm sure you're familiar with it."

I take his hand and rise, managing two steps before I flop, dripping, on the toilet seat. The yellow shag cover presses against my thighs. I adjust the towel around my waist and nod at his last statement—not quite a question.

Is this what it feels like? It's no wonder they call it a miracle drug. Is this how Dad would feel each night as I gave him the dose? Did he get this same wonderful sense of calm, the amazing feeling of wholeness and comfort that comes from having all of your pain whisked away in an instant?

So much of the discussion on the news and everywhere else about Lazarus is about keeping the Undead sane, preventing the outbreaks of violence. Nobody ever talks about this part, the part where it actually makes you feel alive, and what it feels like to be off of it.

"How can you . . . " I hesitate, not sure how to ask the question I want to ask. He watches me with those intent brown eyes and I look away, still feeling exposed despite the towel on my lap.

As if reading my mind—or, at least, my expression—Randy smiles. "I imagine you have a lot of questions, and I'll be happy to answer what I can. But I think, just now, we've got more important things to tend to."

He reaches under the sink, pulling out a Tupperware container, and drops the needle into it. He seals it back up and withdraws a small first aid kit from the cabinet. After a moment of digging around inside, he pulls out a sealed envelope, holding it by the corner. It's about the size and shape of a wrapped condom.

"Suture material," he says, laying it on top of the stack of Ash's clothes sitting by the sink. "You'll want to tie up the edges of these bigger wounds. We do heal, a bit, when we're taking Lazarus, but it's slow and imperfect. Sewing them up will help."

I cringe away from him. He shrugs.

"I mean, I'm not saying you *can't* walk around with gaping

69

wounds. It's your call. I'm just sayin' it's a pain in the ass keeping them clean. You keep getting lint in there, and nobody likes digging cat hair out of their gut."

I adjust the towel across my lap and glance down at my body, which is livid with bruises. My flesh hangs awkwardly over my ribs; several seem broken, jutting out like knobs under the skin.

Randy's unwrapping the suture material and threading the needle. His hands move expertly, and within a moment there's a needle piercing my face, drawing suture material through a wound near my cheekbone. "You're lucky, in a sense. I mean, that's a dick thing to say to someone who's just woken up on the wrong side of the grave, but all things considered, your parts all seem to work. Car accidents get messy. You could've ended up with two shattered legs, or a broken neck, an' then you'd be stuck shuffling around like Quasimodo."

He snips the edges of the suture and prods at my face, testing the stitch.

"Lucky," I echo, when he takes his hand away. I don't feel lucky, but he has a point: I'm not dead. I'm mostly whole. I've got people helping me, for some reason I can't even begin to comprehend. But I'm not dead, and I didn't get picked up like a stray dog and shepherded off to get my ID number. If I hadn't walked away from that accident, they'd be sending a social worker for Zoe right now.

Zoe. Shit. She must be so worried.

"Anyway. You're good to go for now." Randy pats me on the cheek, a patronizing gesture, and backs away. "I'll leave you to get dressed."

He leaves, closing the bathroom door behind him, and I wait for a moment, willing my legs to work properly. I'm afraid that I'll collapse again as soon as I stand.

I lean forward, curling my toes. My brain sends its signals, and I can almost feel the electrical impulses of nerves twitching along my body, accompanying that hyper-awareness of the blood moving through my veins. I stand. Move one foot, then another. Like learning how to walk again, for the first time, but it's all coming back quickly, and within moments I'm standing in front of the sink, staring at myself in the mirror.

My corpse stares back at me.

Ash's clothes are too big in some places, too small in others. The sweatpants ride up above my ankles; the shirt billows like a circus tent. I don't mind. I'm thankful it's not rubbing against my ruined skin, tugging loose stitches or scraping off more flesh.

I step into the hall, the old trailer creaking under my weight, and hesitate. Voices, from the direction of the kitchen. Randy and Ash—and a third, a woman I don't recognize.

"—you're doing," I hear her say.

"What was I supposed to do?" Randy's voice. "Leave him on the side of the road? Let him get picked up by cops or vultures or God knows what else?"

"It's not like you," the woman's saying. "This sentimental side."

"He's not wrong," I hear Ash say.

"Of course you'd say that, Ash," she says. "You've always been like that. Soft-hearted."

I stand awkwardly in the hall, not sure whether to step out and approach them or keep lingering here and risk being seen eavesdropping.

"He'll eat through your Lazarus quick," the woman's saying. I hear a note of resignation in her voice, the tone of someone abandoning an argument she knows she can't win. "So long as you're both honest with yourselves about that. The timing is bad."

"Let me worry about that," Randy says, and his accent has thickened, deepened, the control he puts over it slipping. "An' you just worry 'bout your own self."

I decide that's as good a moment as any to come down the hall. The hallway opens into the small dining area, and Ash and Randy are seated across from each other at a battered old table.

A woman about Ash's age stands at the sink, wiping suds from a dish. She has steel-gray hair and a slight, wiry frame, with the kind of posture that makes you want to stand up a little straighter for fear of reprobation. But when she turns to me, there's kindness in her eyes, and I'm relieved; it's not the kind of response I'd expected.

"Davin, right?" She looks over me, from my bare feet to my rumpled hair, and smiles. "I'm Lilith. Ash's wife. I hope you're feeling a bit better."

"Widow, technically," Randy says. He's sitting backwards in the chair, his arms wrapped casually over the back rest. "Seeing as we Undead don't have those rights anymore. Necrophilia laws, you know."

I pull out a chair, feeling numb, disconnected, as if I'm driving my body like a car from some more remote driver's seat. But it beats the agony of before, so I won't complain.

"The law can kiss my ass," Ash says mildly. "I said 'til death do us part,' and death did no such thing. I'm still here."

"Don't mind my husband." Lilith pulls away from the sink, turning to look through the fridge. She stops, brow furrowing, and closes the refrigerator door, looking questioningly between Ash and Randy. "He's a die-hard romantic."

Die-hard. Ha.

"This is the point where we'd usually offer you something to drink and a bite to eat," Ash explains, turning those faded blue-gray eyes toward me, "but you might not be ready for that yet."

"Ready?"

"Undead don't eat, as a rule," Randy explains. "With enough Lazarus in your system, you can do it—at least, if enough of your guts are intact to allow it—but it's something you have to build up to. Judging by how you looked when I found you, anything that went into your stomach just now would likely end up a bloody stain on Ash's floor, and I don't think Lilith would appreciate that much."

I shake my head, feeling a twinge of nausea at the thought. "No, it's okay. I'm . . . not hungry." Again, I try to clear my throat, to speak in something more than a rasp. "Maybe a glass of water?"

Ash meets Lilith's eyes, and he nods. She reaches up into a cabinet and pulls down a glass, filling it at the sink before handing it to me. I'm surprised at the warmth of her touch, so different from her husband's room-temperature grasp.

And my own.

"So, Davin," Randy says, watching me carefully as I take slow sips. "I promised I would answer your questions, if I can. So. What do you want to know?"

I set the glass down, testing the water's effects. I can feel it trickling down my esophagus, dripping its way through my body like raindrops against a window pane. I try to make sense of the jumble of questions in my mind, deciding which to ask first. "Why did you save me?"

He grins. "I'm not quite sure 'save' is the word, buddy." His eyes lift, training themselves on the ceiling, as if taking a moment to formulate the response. "But. I guess . . . it's lonely, being one of us. Our social circle is rather small." At this, he gestures around the table.

I look at him, waiting for him to drop his eyes. He doesn't, and I study his face, the dark bruise around his exposed throat. He's not telling me everything, I think, but I don't think he's outright lying. I let it go.

Instead, I ask my next most pressing question: "How . . . how is it that you can live like this? I mean . . . "

There are laws and regulations about this sort of thing. The Undead aren't supposed to have houses or wives or property. They're supposed to have caretakers 24/7. They're supposed to be kept in facilities, or monitored all the time by their families.

They're definitely not supposed to be driving sports cars and picking up strays.

"We're unregistered Undead," Ash answers. "Technically, no one knows we've died. Or—let me rephrase that—the government doesn't know. We keep our heads down, and . . . " He trails off, shrugging vaguely. "No dog-catchers."

"It's worth pointing out," Randy adds, "that you'd also fall into that category, if you want to. At this moment, no one outside of this room knows that you're dead, much less Undead."

No one outside of this room.

"I need to get home. I . . . I'll need a ride."

"I figured as much," Ash says, and raises a hand to stop me from babbling on. "We'll get you home. Don't worry about that. We're not holding you prisoner or anything in here, I assure you."

I sense a "but" coming on.

"But I would . . . strongly recommend you stay here and rest a while. You've only got one dose of Lazarus in you, and it'll wear off fast. You have to take some time for it to build up in your system before it'll last. Your body's not going to regenerate at all if you don't take it real easy for a little bit. Trust us on this."

I think about fighting this, but the crackling has started to return to the edges of my vision—those faint black dots, threatening to grow larger. Hints of pain stir in my body, first in my gut, then radiating slowly upward. It's not unbearable, but it is present, and with it comes the specter of exhaustion.

"The Lazarus," I say, trying to hold onto consciousness. I grasp the edges of the table in an effort to steady myself. "If you're not . . . the doctors can't . . . ?"

"We have our own sources," Randy explains with a wry smile. "Anything folks need, there's a way to get hold of somehow. There's a lot more of us out there than you might think."

Of course. I'd always known that unregistered Undead existed, that back alley Lazarus deals were a thing that happened. Sometimes the corpses involved got twice-dead with bullets in their heads. But hearing about it on the news and actually seeing it face-to-face are different.

"Davin? You still with us, kid?" Ash tilts his head, colorless eyes studying my face in concern. "Looks like you zoned out there for a bit."

I nod, mutely, suddenly too exhausted to formulate a

response. I'm so tired. I really need to go home. But I really need to sleep too. I scoot my chair back, and immediately start to slump sideways instead of managing to stand. Randy's at my elbow again, and somehow I find my feet. He nudges me past the table and toward the couch, which has been made up with a threadbare blanket. I collapse onto this, and fall into something not quite like sleep, and stay that way until my senses fade entirely.

There's darkness. And then, something deeper than darkness— a void, an utter nothingness. The absence of light, of sound, of meaning. There's only me, standing on the edge of an abyss, and the terrible realization that I could tip forward at any minute to fall eternally into oblivion.

There's a river in England that seems, on the surface, like a normal mountain stream. I saw a documentary about it once, on the tail end of one of Zoe's news shows. The river is barely six feet wide and seems gentle and calm. But those who fall into it are pulled down into a deep, vicious current, dragged into a jagged ravine, pulled beneath the surface of the shockingly deep waters. Those who fall into the River Strid are sucked down into darkness and never emerge again.

Now, in my dream, I feel as though I'm standing on the banks of that river.

Just one step, just leaning forward a little, and the world will tilt away from me and drop me into a deep chasm. Just one more step, and I'll be swept away into nothingness.

In my body, my chest hitches. My heart strains, pumping with difficulty to circulate sluggish blood through my body. It heaves, and stops. My body, for a moment, is utterly still.

Just one little step, I think. *One little step, and then you'll fall away into oblivion.*

But the feeling of my stopped heart frightens me. It's not time yet. I'm not ready. I throw myself back, forcing my consciousness away from that bottomless void, and suddenly the world bursts back into view around me; the nothingness disappears. My heart resumes its sluggish pounding.

My eyes fly open. Ash's living room rematerializes.

Randy, sitting on a nearby chair, one leg folded over the other, turns dark brown eyes toward me. One brow lifts, the hint of a smirk touching his pale lips. "Well, Davin. Welcome back to the land of the not-quite-living. Guess you made it after all."

I blink at him, uncomprehending, brain fogged over with sleep and death and disorientation. Light filters in through a window, but I can't quite make sense of what it means; something about it looks wrong, like the angle has gone sideways.

"It's mid-afternoon," Randy says, following my gaze to the window. "You slept a long time. Almost 24 hours. We were taking bets on whether or not you'd wake up."

I reach for the couch beneath me, gripping it, grounding myself to the realness of the cushions. I push myself up into a seated position, braced against an elbow, and try to find my voice. "Was that . . . likely?"

"Well, all I'm sayin' is Lilith owes me 20 bucks," Randy says, and his grin broadens but doesn't reach his eyes. "So the Undeath thing is a little touch-and-go. Every once in a while you get a corpse who comes back, walks around, everything's terribly dramatic . . . and then, boom. Nothing. Just keels over and goes right back to being dead. It's a bitch for the family to deal with, obviously, a whole rollercoaster of emotions. But it *has* contributed to the ritual of bringing back the wake, and any excuse to throw back a few drinks sounds like a fine tradition to me."

I know what he's talking about there, at least: since the dead began to rise, holding wakes has become increasingly common. Since a corpse can take anywhere from a few hours to a couple of days to come back, some people have chosen to wait and see if their loved ones come back before moving on with their grief and rituals. Other people are very firm about not wanting to come back as Undead, and they've got it written into their wills that they want to be cremated immediately. There's all these express-crematorium services that popped up overnight to meet that demand, but the wakes are still more common. You hear people talk about it in passing, so-and-so's hairdresser attending a wake for a neighbor's son, that sort of thing. It's just sort of a part of what life looks like now.

The idea that the Undead might hold vigils of their own though, that's news to me. Then again, the idea that Undead might be living on their own and making friends is news to me, too.

"So is it going to be like this every night?" I ask, continuing to force myself upright, shifting my weight to throw my legs off the side of the couch. They each feel like they weigh a thousand pounds, and every inch of my body screams in protest against the effort.

Randy shakes his head. "Probably not. It gets a little better over time, as you adjust. And once you get enough Lazarus in your system, it'll be almost like you never died." He hesitates, glancing over his shoulder a moment, gaze trailing down the hall toward the master bedroom at the end of the trailer. "Speaking of Lazarus, I've got one more dose for you. After this, the charity is over. We'll have to sort out a payment plan. Ash is too much of a coward to say that to your face, so he volunteered me for the job—but anyway. We'll sort it out."

He tosses me a sandwich bag holding a small vial of liquid and a capped syringe. I cradle the bag in open palms, not quite sure if it's a gift I want to accept.

"It's best if you can hit a vein," Randy's saying, "but if you just get it in your body somewhere, it'll still work. More or less. I'll show you how, if you want."

"It's . . . okay. I know how it works," I say, closing my eyes and willing my muscles to work in tandem. I thrust downward, rising to my feet; my nerves begin to respond, sparking off like

77

fireworks across my body. "My dad. He's . . . I gave him his meds. It can't be too different on myself."

Something flickers across Randy's face, some hint of surprise or recognition. "So your dad's Undead?"

"Yeah. He's . . . at the Lazarus House. Was driving home from there when . . . "

"Ah. Well. That does make things easy on you then." A pause. "You got extra in your house then? Hiding out in a medicine cabinet some place?"

"Maybe. I don't remember." I frown, and the expression feels lopsided, my lips tugging downward unevenly thanks to the stitches up one side of my face. "Listen. I . . . thank you. For all this. But I really, really need to get home."

"I figured as much," Randy says, unfolding his legs and rising to his feet as well. Whatever had flickered through his expression before is gone now. His face is a pale, unreadable mask. "Let's get you home then. Lilith probably wants her couch back anyway."

Ash is leaning against the front of the trailer when we leave, smoking a cigarette. Between puffs, he coughs, bent nearly double with the effort. His lungs make a wet, grating sound as the air pushes through them, and I watch with a kind of sick fascination as he coughs up gobs of some dark, viscous liquid. It drips over onto his chin, and he wipes it away with the back of his hand. He catches me watching, and offers a meager half-smile and a few fingertips lifted in a wave.

"Those will kill you, y'know," Randy says.

Ash smirks, ignoring him. His gray eyes settle on me instead. "You heading home then?"

I nod. "Thank you. For the hospitality, and . . . everything."

His eyes dart between me and Randy, something unspoken passing between the two of them, before he looks back my direction. He shrugs. "You're welcome. I'm sure we'll be seeing you again some time."

Despite their kindness, part of me is hoping he's wrong about that. I can't shake the feeling that there's something more going on, some deeper reason for their random generosity—no one is this nice to a stranger, that's just not how the world works—and not knowing what that might be is making me deeply uneasy. But maybe part of my skepticism and reluctance is an unwillingness to accept what's happened to me. Maybe somewhere, deep down, I'm thinking that if I don't let myself get too close to these people, if I don't get too invested in their Undead society, that I might still be able to wake up and realize that all of this has been some kind of terrible dream.

I mutter a farewell and shuffle back to Randy's Mercedes. The interior is streaked with mud and blood, and I grimace at the sight before climbing inside.

"I think I owe you for a car detail," I say as he climbs into the driver's side. "Among other things."

"To be honest, I've always fuckin' hated this car. I kinda like the idea of seeing it be as fucked up as we are."

I wait to see if he explains, and after a long silent moment between us, his eyes roll in a sidelong gaze. He lets out a sigh, but he doesn't explain. Instead he says, with the tonal shift of someone changing the subject, "So, where am I headed?"

I tell him the address, and when his brow furrows, I clarify with landmarks. It takes a few minutes for it to click, like he's trying to map it out in his head.

"You're not from around here, huh?"

He shakes his head. "That obvious, huh?"

I look at him: his pink hair, the expensive clothes, the sports car, that livid bruise seen through the open collar of his button-up. "I didn't peg you for the type who tries too hard to blend in."

"Guilty." He guides the car off the side road and back onto a main street, accelerating smoothly onto the county highway. "I won't bore you with the details, 'cause we ain't got that kind of time. Save it for some longer road trip, maybe." He grins. "But, short version: grew up down south. Family's got a lot of old money, dad's real big in local politics. My death was . . . an embarrassment."

My brows lift. "So he covered it up?"

He nods. "Officially, as far as the government knows, I'm alive and well and on some kind of sabbatical here in the Land of Enchantment." He shrugs. "But he pays the bills to keep me quiet, an' I'm in no hurry to get myself rounded up and dumped in a home someplace, so you won't hear me complaining. Anyway. That's my story. What's yours?"

I hesitate, not sure what feels safe to share. It's odd, being this uneasy about opening up to someone who has gone so far out of his way to help me—but his generosity is one of the things that makes me most uncomfortable. "Mom's dead," I say, finally. "Dad's Undead."

I leave it at that, and after a lull of silence passes over the inside of the car, Randy laughs. "You're a talkative one. A regular chatterbox. Like, seriously, how does anyone ever get a word in edgewise?"

I shrug, and offer him a smile that only twitches at the corner of a lip, and try to think of some newer, safer topic to steer toward. When I can't come up with anything, he takes pity on me and twists the volume knob of the radio, and for a while it's just silence between us with synth-pop filling the gaps, and I'm more than happy to lose myself in the repetitive, heart-like pounding.

When we get close to my house, I tap the passenger window and tilt my head for him to turn. "Here," I say, pointing at the house: its empty driveway, the prickly pear cactus that's taken over the graveled yard, the purple-red fruits growing among the needles. There's a bench on the front porch that my dad made a long time ago, a project with his sponsor when he was still attending AA. Piles of cigarette butts drift around the legs like snow.

The living room windows open over the yard, and I see a dark space open in the blinds, a pair of bespectacled eyes peering out through them. As Randy cuts the engine, I unfold myself from the car and out into the driveway and Zoe—seeing me through the blinds—lets out a shriek loud enough that I can hear it from here. Before I get to the front door, she's run to it, thrown it open, and launched herself out into the driveway. She throws herself against me, pulling me into a desperate hug, temporarily forgetting how utterly uncool she's supposed to find me these days.

My ribs crunch and pop, dislodged by her embrace.

"Jesus fucking Christ on toast, Davin," she says, ignoring or not noticing the grimace that passes over my features at her tight hold. "Where the *fuck* have you been?"

She pulls back and pounds her fist into my chest.

I grunt, gritting my teeth at the pain as her fists drive into my bruised ribs, and catch her hands to stop her.

Behind us, back at the car, Randy slowly climbs out, hanging on the door and lighting himself a cigarette. "Ah," he says. "So that's who you've been in such a hurry to get hold of. Ain't she a little young for you, buddy?"

We both turn to fix him with a dirty look at the same time.

"He's my *brother*, you perv," Zoe says, pulling away from me and looking at Randy, sizing him up. "Who are you?"

"He's . . . " I hesitate, suddenly realizing the full weight of the explanation, and how long and difficult trying to explain all of this will be. "Shit, Zoe, it's a long story. Let's go inside. I . . . have a lot to tell you."

CHAPTER EIGHT

"**IT'S BEEN THREE** days," Zoe's saying, entering full-on mother hen mode. With her wild hair and big sharp eyes, she looks so much like Mom that I get a pang just hearing her nag at me. It's like talking to a ghost. "Where have you been? Seriously? I thought you were dead in a ditch somewhere, I swear to God."

Randy, following us inside uninvited, lets out a snort of laughter.

Zoe's gaze flicks toward him, then to me. Her eyes narrow, suddenly suspicious. "Did the two of you run off together? Who is he? Oh my *God*, Davin, if you've been hiding a secret boyfriend from me—"

Randy chokes, and I shoot him an irritated look as I nudge Zoe back inside and shepherd her toward the living room. I'm struggling to find a gap to get a word in edgewise, because she's still ranting, and Randy's doubled over against the frame of the still-open front door, fighting to regain his composure between wheezing snorts of half-contained laughter.

This is not the way I expected this to go.

Not that I'd ever planned for the moment where I'd have to tell my sister that I was dead. It's not the kind of scenario you expect to be stuck in, even when you're living in a world where corpses still shuffle around and talk. But if I had given it much thought, if I had planned for this moment, I would have anticipated . . . something else.

"Zoe," I say, with some sharpness in my voice to make her pay attention, "this is serious."

She starts to say something, probably some witty comeback,

but stops when she sees my face. Her brow furrows, expression suddenly worried. She's looking at me for the first time, *really* looking, and her gaze traces over the wound on my cheek, the paleness of my skin. Her mouth goes thin, a hard line. She looks like she's bracing for impact.

"Something happened," I say, trying now to keep my voice calm and even. Trying not to let it break, because this whole situation was easier to swallow when I didn't have to say it out loud, when I didn't have to look it in the face and acknowledge that it was really happening. I close my eyes and force air into my lungs, even though the deep breath is now unnecessary, even though breathing now is nothing more than habit and a necessity for speech. "There was an accident."

"At the Lazarus House . . . ?" She sounds scared, and I don't open my eyes. "I tried calling them, to see if they knew where you were or if something had happened to Dad. But nobody would tell me anything because I'm underage. They wouldn't even let me talk to Dad."

I know if I look her in the eye right now, I'm going to start crying, and I don't know whether Undead can cry. It's not something I've ever thought to ask about. I'm half afraid that blood is going to start pooling behind my eyelids, dripping down my cheeks like stigmata. I swallow, another reflex, another vestigial gesture of life.

"No," I tell her, opening my eyes and fixing my gaze on a point a little over her left shoulder so I don't have to look her in the eye. "On my way back."

Silence settles between us, and it's heavy, pregnant with untold details. Randy clears his throat; his clothes rustle as he straightens, the humor having seeped out of him.

" . . . Davin. Where's your car?" Suspicious. Understanding, but not wanting to believe it. Her eyes lift to Randy, who's lingering in the doorway like an awkward specter. "Why did that guy drive you here?"

"I lost control of the car in the rain," I said. "I hydroplaned off the bridge over the Animas."

Her gaze snaps back to me, eyes narrowed suspiciously. "But . . . you're okay?"

I try to smile. It falters.

Zoe lifts a hand to cover her mouth, eyes going wide, and she's rendered momentarily speechless. Behind her dark eyes, I can practically see the thoughts processing, running through her brain like lines of code. I imagine them, all the ones and zeroes, computational figures, flickering digits.

Randy slides outside, but doesn't close the door. I hear the flick of a lighter, smell the scent of a freshly-lit cigarette as he smokes on the front porch.

"That's Randy," I say, nodding in his general direction. "He, uh, found me. After. Helped me get cleaned up. Gave me . . . " I hesitate, mouth not wanting to form words. "Lazarus."

I reach into my pocket, then, for the vial and the capped syringe he sent me home with, and hold them out for Zoe as if seeing them would in any way make it easier to understand or accept.

She leans across the couch and hugs me. The gesture takes me off-guard; I'm expecting her to start crying or get angry, but she's just wrapping her arms around me, and her expression when she pulls away is one of happiness—relief. "I'm glad you're okay."

I'm not, though, and I just stare at her, not sure how I can explain, not sure how it is that she's not grasping this. I'm dead. That's pretty much the definition of not okay.

Maybe she sees this in my eyes, because her smile twists, an ironic curve at the edge of the lips. "I mean, not *okay*, but... You're here. You came back. I get to talk to you."

Until this moment, it never occurred to me that that might be something to celebrate.

"So."

Silence has settled over the house like snow, and when it becomes clear that nobody else is eager to break it, I take it upon myself to try. I'm not sure how you continue a conversation after dropping a bombshell like "oh hey, guess what, I'm dead now." I'm not sure if your life can ever be normal again. But I want it to be—I need it to be. "What have *you* been up to?"

Zoe's brows rise, and she tugs at a strand of curly hair, wrapping it nervously around a finger. She looks like she's on the edge of laughter, or maybe about to start yelling at me again, more mother-hen nagging. Something bright and dangerous is shining in her eyes. "I guess you haven't been watching the news?"

"I've been a little busy."

"I mean, obviously. But Davin, it's been *crazy*. Everything's gone to shit in the last couple of days."

This seems to catch Randy's attention. He's been lingering in the kitchen, trying not to look at us while we catch up, as if he were caught witnessing something intimate. He's been rifling through cabinets and pawing disinterestedly at canned goods, but he stops, a can of store-brand refried beans in his hand. He has the eavesdropper expression, sharp-focused eyes and mouth slightly parted in concentration.

Zoe ignores him. Instead, she reaches for the coffee table and grabs the remote, flicking on the television. She scrolls through recorded programming, selects one of several news broadcasts she's recorded over the past few days. This isn't new—she tends to DVR all of the Undead-related news so she can pick it apart later—but there's a fresh urgency in her movement, like a gumshoe detective who can't wait to reveal the solution to the mystery.

The television shows an image of a large, mostly black German shepherd straining at the end of a leash, jaws open, tongue lolling over large white teeth. The voiceover starts.

"Undead-sniffing dogs? An innovative program launched in select Arizona police precincts is investigating that possibility."

The newscaster reads his teleprompter with the lilt of a human interest piece, that tone where you report the wacky hijinks of a donkey-stealing drunk man or some other tidbit of weird news. Zoe glances between me and the screen, then back, watching my face for a reaction. She rapidly taps the volume button on the remote, turning up the sound.

"Dogs can be trained to identify all sorts of specific olfactory cues," someone with a microphone shoved in their face is saying. "We have dogs that can identify bombs, dogs that can find drugs and contraband, even dogs that can detect cancer cells. It's really not a stretch to think that dogs could be useful in identifying Undead."

A newscaster voiceover in that same false, cheery voice: "Authorities say that the dogs may be revolutionary in identifying cases of Undead attempting to circumvent the laws of the Undead Registration Act, which may be a cause behind the recent reports of violence among certain populations."

"It's a matter of public safety." The camera cuts to someone wearing a police uniform. "We have to know who these people are, so that appropriate safety precautions can be taken to protect the citizens of Arizona as well as the Undead populations. Most of these people have been very compliant with following the rules; we're not worried about them. It's the ones slipping through the cracks, causing trouble, that we're out to catch."

The screen changes, the newscaster reading a different set of prompts for a different story, and Zoe hits pause, exits, goes back to scrolling through recordings.

"Won't be long until that finds its way across state lines," Randy says. He's left the kitchen, is standing now behind the couch. He leans forward, resting his elbows on the back of the couch; in one hand, he's still holding the can of beans, though he doesn't seem to notice it. "You know, they bred wolf hybrids specifically to hunt and attack resistors during South African apartheid? Maybe folks in Arizona will get lucky an' find a bit of the old stock. Wouldn't that be somethin' to see."

He sounds amused, unconcerned. I wish I could share the sentiment. In my mind, all I can see are snarling dogs tearing at flesh that will never heal. All I can think of are dogs barking and snarling at my door, people in uniform dragging me outside.

"Wait," Zoe says grimly, pulling up another recording. "It gets worse."

"SPECIAL REPORT!"

The voice is loud, a staccato burst against the silence. I jump, startled.

"We interrupt this program to bring you a live, important health update!" The screen is time-stamped with yesterday's date.

There's suddenly a flurry of action on the screen, and it takes my sluggish brain a moment to catch up with everything, to make sense of what I'm even seeing and hearing.

Footage of an Undead woman, backed into the corner of an alleyway. She's wearing tattered clothes and has a wild, manic look in her eyes, like an animal. Her lips are curled back in a snarl, more dog than human. There's a dark stain on her shirt, blood or something like it; yellowing exposed bone is visible along her collarbone.

The voiceover is saying: "A public health crisis has been declared. Due to multiple reports nationwide of violence erupting among the Undead community, the World Health Organization believes it is no longer possible to entrust these individuals with their own treatment."

Subconsciously, I roll the bottle of Lazarus in my hand between my fingertips, feeling its cool glass sides through the plastic bag. My eyes stay glued to the screen, and something achy and throbbing starts up in my chest—my heart trying to pound, a sluggish echo of the panic response.

"These people are sick," someone's saying. He's tall, reedy, professorial. The caption suggests he's with the CDC. "We're not here to say they don't need help or compassion. We're saying that the stresses of caring for Undead are too great to place on family members, and the risks are just too high. We believe that the reports of violence we've seen are directly tied to poor outpatient care. That's why we strongly urge that every Undead in the country immediately check themselves into a professionally-staffed Lazarus House for inpatient treatment."

The image changes, this time to dash-cam footage from a police car. You can see the officer trying to talk to someone with pale skin and a matted tangle of hair. You can't tell whether they're male or female, but you can see the signs of Undeath— the paleness of the skin, the papery quality of the flesh shifting over ruined muscles. The Undead lunges, and the officer lifts his gun. Two shots to the chest, and the Undead just keeps coming, hands outstretched. The third bullet strikes home, hitting the Undead square in the forehead, and the skull snaps back, the body making a perfect arc as it swings backward and strikes the pavement. A spatter of blood and fluid fans out on the concrete.

"These horrifying images represent a growing trend that has been worrying officials across the country," the voiceover is saying. "The Undead have become increasingly violent and erratic in their behavior."

"This is such bullshit," Zoe's saying, but I wave a hand to silence her so I can hear. I realize I've pulled forward, leaning toward the TV like my body's being drawn into it. I'm literally at the edge of my seat, and the tension running through my body is so tight I worry about the muscles tearing free of their bones.

There's a person on the TV now, a balding guy who seems familiar. The caption below him reads that he's the head advising doctor at the New Mexico Lazarus House.

"Obviously, we are concerned about these reports," he's saying. "The safety of our patients is our utmost concern, but we are also concerned for the well-being of our community. The Undead need specialized treatment that the average person simply cannot provide. If you are taking care of an Undead, we urge you to call for help from our facility right away."

"*Well,*" Randy says, his voice lilting with ironic amusement. "Won't be long 'til they've legislated that. I give 'em a month, tops, 'til Undead are rounded up an' imprisoned. I mean"—he lifts his fingers to make quote signs in the air—"put into treatment facilities."

~~

Zoe flips through a few more recordings, all of them touching on the same themes: violence has exploded among the Undead, the Undead aren't taking their Lazarus, and their families can't take care of them. They need to go into treatment facilities. Different channels spin the story in different ways, but they're all telling the same narrative.

"It's bullshit," Randy says. "Just propaganda. Undead aren't any more violent than ever, an' that's not very much. Fewer dead folks cause trouble than living ones anyway."

Zoe turns her eyes toward him, and something eager shines in them. She hadn't paid much attention to him before, but now she's honed in on him like a heat-seeking missile. She's looking at him with the kind of awe she used to have for me—that "my big brother is so cool" look. She's looking at him like he's a superhero, this stranger who saved her brother and shares her opinions on Undead politics.

"Right?" she says. "That's what I've been saying. It doesn't make any sense."

My head is aching, brain reeling with too much information, conflicting emotions. I'm exhausted and overloaded. Being dead, now Undead, is enough to try and process; I can barely keep up with their banter as they go back and forth.

"If it's going off Lazarus," Randy's saying, leaning hard into the back of the couch so he can bend in close, his pale face between us, "why would the violence be getting *worse* now? Sure, I can see a few people going off their meds, but no way there's an epidemic like this. The whole thing smells like a setup."

"Exactly!" Zoe's head bobs excitedly, dark curls dancing around her shoulders. "If anything, you'd think things would have been worst when the epidemic was brand new and nobody knew how to treat it. Or else the entire violence narrative is completely made up."

Randy shrugs, a theatrical sweeping gesture made only

slightly ridiculous by the can of beans in his right hand. "And meanwhile, they're out on the streets rounding us up like strays. Cramming us in their so-called treatment center—and for what, I wonder? If you ask me, this whole thing is a ploy. A way to smoke us out of our holes like goddamn rabbits."

"Do you really think so?" I shift my position on the couch, feeling suddenly restless. My fingers curl around the dose of Lazarus in my hand, suddenly uneasy. The TV is paused on the Undead woman, her wild-eyes and bared teeth. "Are you saying they're faking this?"

He lifts dark eyes to meet mine, pushing away from the back of the couch. He looks away suddenly, training his attention on the ceiling, beginning to pace in small, agitated circles in the small living room. "Shit, Davin. You think a government that don't mind rounding us up an' dropping us into a prison camp to die is really above manufacturing a health scare to keep us toeing the line?"

"It's not a prison camp." I can't believe I'm defending the Lazarus House. "It's . . . "

"A treatment facility?" He scoffs. "Bullshit. We're *dead*, Davin. What the fuck are they treating? Do you see folks going in there and coming out *better*?"

"No, but—"

"Best case scenario, you go in there so you can be dead without anybody havin' to look at you. But this mandatory treatment thing? Bullshit. They want an excuse to do something to people behind closed doors. Maybe they're gonna send their inmates somewhere else, put 'em to work. Take advantage of a workforce that never gets tired, never eats, doesn't have to get paid. Or maybe they're shooting 'em up with drugs like goddamn lab rats. But I guarantee they're up to something."

It wouldn't be hard to imagine losing control, turning into some kind of animal.

A person in the highway, crouched over the carcass of an animal. Headlights washing over its slender body, meat and gore dripping from its open mouth.

The memory hits me like a ton of bricks—a moment easily forgotten in the horror that followed, but now here it is, demanding audience in my brain. I saw that, right? It wasn't a hallucination? I strain, trying to remember, trying to make sense of those moments before my death and untangle them from the hallucinogenic dreamscape that followed.

But Randy and Zoe aren't paying attention to me; they're back to trading conspiracy theories, pinging off each other's thoughts like old friends, and suddenly I'm exhausted. The exhaustion threatens to pull me under, like the swift current of a river, and I drag myself to my feet, muttering some excuse as I start down the hall for my bed. The thoughts swirling around and ricocheting through my brain have grown so loud that they're drowning each other out; it's all buzzing white noise up there, television static in my head.

From the hall, I can still hear the two of them talking in low, excited voices—kindred spirits finding each other in the desert.

Randy's gone by morning. I wake up to a quiet house, silent except for the sounds of gentle snoring from Zoe's bedroom. In the kitchen, a note's been left on the fridge, written on the back of an envelope; the corner is tucked under a magnet. It says, in neat, squared-off handwriting:

I put my number in your sister's phone, since yours is MIA. But if you need it, here it is again. Call me if you need anything.

Beneath that, the phone number, and Randy's name, signed with less care than the rest of the note—a signature of loops and angles, as if created separately from the rest of his handwriting, as much an artifice as his attempts to cover his accent. I take the note, folding it awkwardly and stuffing it into my pocket.

My lungs are burning, like they're working double-time to get half as much oxygen. Something deep in my gut shifts and groans, like a tearing, gnawing pain, the pain of something coming loose inside.

I make my way back to the hall bathroom, pulling the Lazarus from the drawer where I'd hidden it the night before. I look down at it, willing my hands to stop shaking with anticipation. I don't want to take it, but I don't want to risk being like those people on the TV, even if Randy and Zoe are right and the whole thing isn't even true. I don't want to need this drug, because needing it means that being Undead is real, permanent, a fact of my life.

But I *do* need it, and trembling with pain and withdrawals in the bathroom isn't going to stop that from being true.

The needle pierces my flesh, and I depress the plunger, driving the drug toward the vein in my arm. The vein rolls sideways, and I miss, the needle digging deep into the flesh at the crook of my elbow. But it's close enough to get the job done. It takes just a few seconds for the drug to take effect, and the results are swift and dramatic. It's like coming up for air after being submerged, like that first puff of a cigarette after you've quit for weeks.

Blood rushes through me, leaving me dizzy. I sway and grip the counter with both hands to steady myself, bowing my head over the sink and sucking in deep breaths to fill my lungs.

The trembling inside me stills. My mind goes quiet, peaceful.

Then, for a moment—a fleeting second—I feel something different, something new. Something like hunger. Something like anger. That hesitant moment before you snap and lunge and scream. An urge to tear and shred and destroy.

The urge to kill.

My hands are trembling, and I can't tell if it's from fear or anger or the slow afterburn of the drug making its way through my body. My thoughts are gaining clarity; it's like everything in my mind is suddenly awake, just as everything in my body feels suddenly alive.

I think: *What the fuck was that?*

And then I think, just as quickly: *It was nothing. Don't tell anyone. Don't think about it. You just imagined it. That's all. That has to be all.*

~

I can't get past the weird self-consciousness that I might smell like a corpse, no matter how much I tell myself it's not true. Dad never smelled, really, no more than he stank when he was alive. But all the same, I linger in the shower, scrubbing gently, pondering over the dangers of exfoliating when your skin might not grow back. I spritz on too much cologne. I feel like a tool.

Zoe's awake by the time I get out of the shower. The red bulb over the door is dark. Her bedroom door's closed, but I can hear the rapid click of keys as she pounds away at a keyboard, typing swiftly, enthusiastically. The sound of debate. I hesitate outside her door. Knock. Wait for a response. Nothing. Knock again. Speak through the door. "Zoe?"

Her answer is a monosyllable grunt, not quite a word.

Her joy at seeing me alive—well, alive enough—has clearly faded; we're back to the status quo now. At least one of us adjusts quickly. I consider leaving her be, decide against it. "Can I come in?"

Another grunt. It sounds affirmative. I let myself in.

Her room is a mess, notebooks and books scattered over the floor, energy drink cans piled high on the carpet beside an overflowing trash can. It looks like she's been busy while I was gone. Distracting herself from my unnerving absence? Keeping up with the storm-cloud bursts of the news cycle? Maybe a little of both.

She's still wearing her pajamas, and her hair is a mess, sticking up on one side. But sleepiness is long gone from her eyes; she's alert and hawkish, scanning the computer screen with the kind of ferocity you'd expect from a hungry predator prowling the edges of a flock of sheep. The glow of the screen reflects back in her glasses. There are multiple tabs open, as usual, and she's clicking between them swiftly, too fast for me to get a clear look at any of them.

"What are you doing?"

"There's this forum," she says, clicking over into another window before finally leaning back in her chair, inclining her head toward me. "It has information, without the media bullshit. I wanted to see if anyone had new comments on what's been happening on the news."

"The Lazarus House and everything?"

"Yeah. The *media* went public with everything just recently," she says, and there's something undeniably smug in her voice, "but someone else has to know more than what they're saying."

"Oh." I try to think of something to add. All this time, since Dad died, she's been immersed in searching for answers, in understanding the Undead phenomenon. Now here I am, freshly among the Undead, as clueless as ever about what it really means. I'm a little surprised; you'd think I'd be hungry for answers now too, but all I'm feeling is tired.

She must take my exhaustion as confusion, because she explains: "It's like WikiLeaks for zombies."

"I've never heard of it." I glance over her shoulder at the collection of tabs, the bald hypertext of the pages. It looks like the internet circa 1997.

"You wouldn't. It's deep web stuff." Again, it's impossible to hide the smugness in her voice—the pride. "It's taken me ages to find this much, and I know there's a lot more underneath, if I can get down into it."

"The people—the ones you're talking to—they don't know who you are, do they?"

She turns all the way around at this to shoot me a disparaging look. "Davin. Please. I have proxies set up. I'm under, like, five layers of encryption. I know what I'm doing."

I have only a dim idea of what the fuck she's talking about, so I decide to trust her on that.

"Right." I heave a sigh, feel something loose crackling in my chest. "I'm going to go to the gas station. See if I can talk to my boss and try to hold onto my job. Buy some smokes. You need anything?"

She starts to shake her head, then hesitates. "More Red Bull?"

I smile. It's comforting, in a way, how normal all of this is—how casually she's taking my status as freshly Undead. Maybe it's denial. But it makes me feel better, gives me space to pretend that everything is normal after all, and I wrap myself in that feeling like an old blanket.

I'm halfway out the door when I remember: no car. Right. My piece of shit Toyota is sitting on the banks of the Rio de Animas. Briefly, I think about calling Randy, but dismiss the idea out of hand. I'm not calling him to drive me like a child, to play chauffeur while I run errands and try to put the pieces of my life together. I'm dead, but I'm not helpless.

I start walking.

CHAPTER NINE

IT TAKES ME two hours to walk to work. By the time I reach the gas station, my legs have gone numb. I can vaguely feel bits of flesh worn loose at the soles of my feet, shifting around inside my shoes; what would have once been blisters is now a layer of skin that will never grow back.

I discover, also, that I am no longer employed.

The owner is, naturally, nowhere to be found. My former shift manager makes it pretty clear, though, that not only am I no longer employed, but I'm unwelcome on the premises. Maybe he thinks I'm going to make a scene. He hands me an envelope with my last paycheck in it and stares me down, repeating words like "corporate policy" and "no call, no show." Keeps shaking his head when I try to explain myself—but without a doctor's note, I'm SOL, and I can't very well go to the doctor without making it pretty damn clear that I've checked out of the land of the living.

"I'm really sorry, Davin." Jo, at least, is kind, even if she can't do anything about it. She's working a new schedule, or maybe covering a shift—it's strange seeing her in full daylight. Her complexion is warmer, more coppery, in natural light; or maybe I'm just so used to looking at corpses lately that the blush of life throws me off guard.

"Right." I grit my teeth. Consider, briefly, going to my boss, begging for my job back. But I can't imagine how that conversation would go. There's nothing I can say to him that would change his mind, not without giving myself away in the process.

We're standing outside the Kwik-Gas, smoking. The gas

station is, as usual, mostly deserted, a few customers filling their tanks at the self-service pumps.

"Hey, did you *walk* here?"

"Yeah . . . " I trail off, hesitate, debating what to tell her. She is, after all, the closest thing I have to a friend. "Got into an accident. Totaled the car."

"Aw, shit, are you okay?" She squints at me, as if assessing for damage. Her eyes linger on the inexpertly-stitched wound on my face.

" . . . Yeah. I mean. I didn't go to the hospital or anything." That's true, at least.

She makes a maternal clucking noise, shakes her head sympathetically. "What a shitty thing to have happen though. You total your car and lose your job in the same week? That's got to suck."

"Yep."

She brushes back the long half of her faux-hawk, taking a drag of her cigarette with the other hand. "Tell you what. I'll at least get you a ride home, if that's okay? I'm almost done here. Just hang out for a bit, and I'll take you when I get off."

She heads back inside without waiting on a response, and I linger under the eaves to light another cigarette and consider the offer. I've relied a lot on charity these past few days, but I don't guess I'm in any place to start turning that down.

I do, however, have a little time to kill. I decide to take my shredded feet on one more adventure, an errand to test the mettle of my independence.

Randy had left me with a final dose of Lazarus—the dose I took today. In Dad's medicine cabinet, I found more, enough for a couple of weeks if I'm careful. But he still had some refills; I think, maybe, I could just keep filling the prescriptions, keep myself dosed while staying under the radar, no outside help required.

I've used the same pharmacist for years, even before Dad

died. It's a little neighborhood place, an independent pharmacy run by one old man and a rotating staff of assistants who rarely stay more than a few months before moving on to some place bigger, some place with health insurance and paid time off. I picked the place on a whim, choosing a location close to work out of convenience, since I was always stopping in to pick up medication for Mom during the later stages of her life.

Later, when Dad died, the pharmacist was one of the only people who knew; even though we didn't really know each other, the fact that he was privy to my family secret was enough to foster something like friendship.

His name is Andy. I don't know a last name; I only know Andy from his name tag, even though we've seen each other once a month for about three years.

He's an older guy, well past the age of retirement. I like to imagine that he's still working here in his pharmacy out of love, a real passion for the job, but it's probably more likely that he can't afford to keep a roof over his head on Social Security. He's short, white, balding up top with tufts of gray-white hair over his ears; he has the friendly, open face of a television grandpa. The kind of guy you'd hire to play Santa Claus for the neighborhood kids.

"Ah, Mr. Montoya," he says by way of greeting. He recognizes me before I hand him the paper—the refill order for Dad's last month of Lazarus. Normally, being recognized would make me happy. Now it makes me painfully aware of how much danger I'm in of being found out.

My throat's dry, closed off, and my greeting comes out as more of a squeak. I've never had much of a poker face.

Andy looks up, eyes narrowing behind the crescent frames of his reading glasses. "You feeling under the weather, son? You look a little pale."

Reflexive panic bubbles up, the feeling of being caught out, seen through. I try my best to hide it, my eyes straying from his kindly gaze. "Fine. Little summer cold."

"I hear that's going around," he says, conversationally, but there's a shrewd look in his eye. "You be sure to get some bed rest."

He takes the prescription from me and taps something into the computer. He frowns. "That's funny. It says here your father has already been transferred to the Lazarus House. They've changed his primary care doctor in the system and everything. You shouldn't have to fill your scripts here anymore."

I try to arrange my face into an expression of confusion. "No?"

My brain hums, trying desperately to come up with a believable lie, some sort of explanation or rationalization that will make sense of my request. But the only thing coming up is white noise static, like the inside of my head is a radio tuned to a distant station.

"I can't fill this," Andy continues, filling in the silence. "Worth more than my job to do that—they're cracking down hard on under-the-table sellers. Apparently there's quite a trade in Lazarus on the street, although I can't imagine why. I suppose kids will try to get high off of anything."

Does he suspect me? His expression is just as placid and neutrally friendly as ever, but the fear is hammering my languid heart into action all the same. I swallow, try to find enough saliva in my mouth to moisten my throat. Lick my lips. Try to speak without my voice cracking this time: "I must have misunderstood what the doctor was telling me to do with the refills." I hope I sound confident, convincing. "I'll talk to him."

The pharmacist's eyes fill with paternal concern. I'm glad he doesn't seem to have caught on to my ruse, but I wish he'd stop being so nice; lying to him is making me uncomfortable. "I can call for you and clear this up . . . "

"No, no, it's okay. Don't worry about it."

I turn and go before he has the chance to say anything more, leaving the prescription in his hand.

So much for trying to get my own Lazarus supply.

It's storming out. The humidity has rendered the swamp cooler useless, and the heat inside is sweltering. Standing in the kitchen, prodding idly at a pan of reheated beans, I have a paranoid suspicion that I've started to smell. I imagine my corpse festering in the summer heat, flesh oozing and liquefying. I imagine flesh melting sideways off the bone like putty.

I step back from the stove, lifting my forearm surreptitiously, sniffing at my skin. I can't tell whether it smells like anything. I just know that I *feel* dead; I feel rotten, like an overripe pumpkin that's started to crumple in on itself after being left outside.

I have a momentary absurd urge to dump out the food. *Maybe Zoe should be cooking for herself now,* I think. *Maybe it's not sanitary having a corpse in the kitchen.*

The scent of beans and lard and garlic wafts upward from the pan, hanging in the still hot air of the house. I probably used too much garlic. The scent seems overpowering, and something deep in my ruined guts turns over, a lazy rumbling. They used to rub garlic over the bodies of the dead in some countries, back in the day when they were afraid of vampires. Anointing corpses with garlic and oil and various herbs, basting corpses like some pungent Thanksgiving turkey, all in hopes of keeping the dead in the ground where they belonged.

It's hard, now, to write that off as absurdity.

Maybe the dead coming back to life isn't such a new thing. Maybe this used to happen, before, and they found some way to stop it for years and years, some esoteric knowledge lost to time.

"Ahh, something smells good in here." Zoe's emerged from the hallway. The fog on her glasses and the damp pulled-back hair suggest she must have been in the shower. Moisture—water or sweat—glistens along her brow and the back of her arms. "What's for dinner?"

"Beans and rice."

"Tortilla?"

"Check the fridge."

She obediently makes her way toward it, staring a long while as if expecting more food to materialize within it, or maybe she's just soaking up the cold air again. I'm about to get on her ass about that, go on another fruitless debate about thermodynamics and the electric bill, when she shuts the door and tosses down a package of flour tortillas on the counter.

The normalcy of all of this, the routine of it, makes me want to cry. I feel like screaming at her: *I'm dead, don't you get it, everything is different now.* But for her, it's like nothing ever changed.

"Toast it on the burner?" She nudges the bag of tortillas at me while I start scooping beans and rice onto a plate. "The microwave tastes funny."

"Oh, for fuck's sake. You can toast your own tortilla."

"You do it better," she little-sister wheedles. "I always burn my fingers."

"Fine." I turn the heat down, shifting the pan off the burner and dropping the tortilla down over the open flame, letting it char on one side, then grasp the edge with my fingertips and flip it. I repeat this a couple of times, trying to spread out the toasted char.

The flames lick at my fingers, and I realize I can't feel it. I draw my hand away, shutting off the gas to the burner, before the skin can start to sizzle. My fingertips are shiny, the edges burnt but not reddened; I guess my body's defense systems aren't up to that task. Quickly, before Zoe can notice, I fold up the tortilla and toss it on her plate, handing it over to her and nodding toward the kitchen table.

"You're not going to eat?"

"Zoe."

"I know, I know." She looks up at me, then down at the empty chair at the table.

The table's been set for two for a long time. It had never even occurred to me to try giving Dad anything to eat. The doctors said that he didn't need to eat anymore, and I just believed them, because they were doctors and it seemed to make sense. And maybe, selfishly, because I didn't want to spend any more money than I had to on groceries; maybe it was just easier to cut that line from the budget.

But Undead can eat, sometimes. That's what Ash and Randy had said, right? With enough Lazarus in my system?

I look down at the remaining food in the pan. It smells good, if over-garlicky. I think it might be worth a shot, so I pile a little spoonful of beans and a little spoonful of rice onto a plate, a meager nibble, like what you'd feed to a weaning infant.

Zoe's practically beaming at me as I settle in to eat.

Food is . . . tasteless. I can smell the garlic, and recognize that I should be able to taste it, but my tongue is occupied with the texture. I don't think I've ever really paid attention to the texture of refried beans before; the mealy grittiness of them, the individual pieces of minced garlic sticking out like broken bits of tooth. It's unpalatable, and I push the meal away after my first spoonful, frowning down at my plate.

In the movies, all the zombies eat brains or flesh. We're supposed to be ravenous, mindless killing machines driven by hunger. They used to say that about sharks too, so I guess things change.

My mind flashes back, though, to that night on the bridge; that figure crouched over the animal in the road. It was only the briefest of glimpses; I have no idea what I really saw. Maybe it was nothing. Maybe my memory's all fucked up from being dead. Maybe I just skidded on wet concrete and went over the bridge for no reason and my mind thought up some excuse for it later.

What I do know: ten minutes after eating my spoonful of food, I'm sprawled over the toilet, heaving up bits of brackish bile and blood and God knows what else, painting the toilet bowl red-black with my insides while Zoe pats me on the back and apologizes, over and over, for convincing me to try eating.

She suggests, hopefully, that maybe it was the garlic.

~

For the next two weeks, I try my best to return to something resembling a normal life, even though I know it's an artifice. After Jo dropped me off that one day, she left me with her number in case I needed anything: the second lifeline, the second charitable number that I never planned to call.

I've been taking Dad's Lazarus, and it's been working out okay. No more strange, violent urges; just the occasional pass of hunger, a pang of craving as my ruined guts realize how much they miss food. Otherwise, the worst part of the day is the boredom, the cabin fever.

For two weeks, my days have been filled with domestic tasks. Cleaning, more out of nervous habit than need. Counting out Lazarus, trying to stretch doses, taking as little as I can to get through the day. Calculating expenses and searching online for more work, a cheap car, something—anything—that could break this stand-off with bad luck.

For two weeks, I've waited for authorities to come and find me—moving through each day with the paranoid certainty that I'd open the door to find uniformed officers or lab coat-wearing scientists standing on my doorstep. But there's only silence, underscored by persistent creeping dread.

Soon it'll be the end of the month, and we'll get Dad's Social Security check, and it might be just enough for me to buy a piece of shit junker off Craigslist and try to get my "life" back together.

But first, I have to make it that far—and I'm honestly not sure whether or not that will happen. The Lazarus is running low, and my budgeted ration doesn't seem to be cutting it.

I don't tell Zoe. I don't want to worry her. Besides, I think I might be okay. At first, anyway, it isn't so bad at all. Just a vague, itchy restlessness, the same sort of quiet nagging as nicotine withdrawal. I smoke twice as much, and it goes away for a little while; the nicotine compensates, and I can tell myself that I'll be fine.

But by the morning of day three, I feel sick—weak like the flu. Shaky, that kind of deep trembling that accompanies heavy fever. I stay in bed, staring up at the ceiling without seeing anything, my thoughts a disconnected jumble of images and ideas.

I remember reading somewhere about the diseases carried by corpses. Not just the usual pestilence of rot and decay, but real illness. The things that kill you, after all, can linger in the body, pass on to those around you. I think I remember hearing somewhere that corpses can carry particularly brutal infections, particularly strong pathogens. That the germs you pick up as an undertaker will leave you gravely ill.

Gravely. Ha, ha.

My thoughts drift, foggily, undercut only by the pain.

The pain starts like fire in my gut. It's a tearing, agonizing ache, worse even than the feeling of waking from death; worse than the feeling of puking up gobbets of flesh from deep down inside. Beads of sweat tinged with blood pool on my skin, staining the sheets with smears of crimson.

I think, finally, of calling for Zoe, but by now I can't speak. The pain is too severe, paralyzing in its intensity; my throat is dry and closed, forcing me into silence.

All I can do is sleep, so that's what I do.

I doze intermittently, falling in and out of dreams. The world slips, less solid, flickering like a mirage at the edges of my vision. Time fractures and distorts.

I remember being sick once, as a kid. Some viral bug or another. The heavy fever is the only thing that sticks out in my mind. At the time, Mom was sick herself—battling cancer for the first time, before remission—and I hadn't wanted to disturb her and Dad. I hadn't wanted to burden either of them with my problems, and so I'd tried to care for myself so I wouldn't hog their attention.

I went to bed, sweaty and shivering. No one seemed to notice. For hours, I lay there, trembling beneath the blankets, my parents wrapped up in the selfishness of their worry. I tried to sleep, but my thoughts only wandered, holding my consciousness captive.

But some time late in the night, the door opened and Zoe—little more than a toddler, maybe three or four years old—tip-toed inside. She was holding a stuffed bear against her pajama-clad chest, and the glass bead eyes caught the light, reflected it back on me as if it were alive.

"You going to die?"

"Don't be stupid."

Dying was a thing that both of us knew about far too young, even if she didn't really understand what it meant. It was a word in the household lexicon though, whether we wanted it to be or not. It was a looming specter of possibility, where Mom was concerned.

Zoe came up to the side of my bed, looking nervous and out of place. Usually when she snuck into my room at night it was for her comfort, not mine. She usually crept in here after having a nightmare, or hearing some strange noise that she was certain was a monster. Now the situation had flipped, and she didn't seem to know what to do with herself.

I slid over toward the wall, leaving some space in the twin-size bed for her. Despite the dampness of the sweat-soaked sheets, she crawled up into bed and fitted herself against me, the bear nestled down between us.

"I won't let you die," she said, solemnly. "I watch you."

She did.

By morning, my fever had broken. I felt better, through the worst of it. I got in trouble for hiding the illness; Dad had spanked me, leaving my ass sore and pink, and then felt guilty about it and bought me and Zoe both Push Pops from the gas station. At the time, that had felt like a reasonable enough trade.

What a stupid thing to remember, I think hazily.

What a silly memory to hold onto.

I'm woken by the absence of pain.

It's like losing a heavy blanket in the night. The weight of pain lifts and for a moment it's like my body goes with it; a sensation of weightlessness, of emptiness, as if the pain were the only thing chaining me to the world. I feel like a ghost, bodiless and untethered.

Slowly, piecemeal, my senses return, consciousness settling back into my body. I'm aware of the feeling of sheets beneath my fingers, the softness of the mattress, the dimly-lit room around me, hints of light peeking around the edge of the curtains.

Randy, leaning over me. Pale skin picking up bluish tones in the darkness of the room. The faintest hint of a smile lingers at the corner of his lips, but his dark eyes are solemn.

This can't be real, I think, blinking up at him.

What's he doing here? How did he get here? It's all too familiar. It's got to be a memory, another dream.

But Zoe is hovering behind him, standing on her toes to peek over his shoulder. She tugs nervously at her hair. Her face has the puffy, flushed look of someone who's been crying.

"We've got to stop meeting like this," Randy says dryly. He draws back from my bedside, and as he moves I can see the empty syringe in his hand.

"Davin, I'm sorry. Don't be mad." Zoe's wide-eyed. Her hair is more disheveled than usual. I'm not used to seeing her like this; she's been cool-headed and independent for so long that I've let myself forget that she's just a kid. And right now, a terrified kid. "I thought you were dying. I didn't know who else to call."

My gaze travels back to Randy, now lingering at the doorway as if contemplating making an escape.

But I can't die, I think numbly, barely able to stop the words from coming out. *I'm already dead.*

CHAPTER TEN

I **STRUGGLE TO** find my feet, my knees wobbling and threatening to collapse under my weight. The pain is gone, replaced by a strange anxiousness. I feel disconnected from my body, like wires are loose somewhere and the signals sent from my brain take too long to process.

My sheets are soaked through with blood and sweat.

It's been two days since I first went to bed. Two days lost to that dream-addled state of fever and withdrawal. I had no idea. I can barely remember anything, just snatches of time.

Zoe had tried, she insisted, to let me sleep it off. She didn't know, of course, that I hadn't been taking my Lazarus, or—more accurately—that the dose hadn't been high enough to prevent withdrawal from kicking in. If she'd known, she might have acted differently. Might not have left me to sleep for so many hours.

I guess she tried to wake me up. I guess she came in and saw me lying there in a puddle of blood and sweat, not breathing, unresponsive, and panicked. She said she got halfway through dialing 911 before she remembered I was a corpse now, that paramedics wouldn't do anything to save me. She called Randy and hovered in the hall, pacing and waiting and panicking.

It must have been awful for her. It must have been terrifying.

She's still convinced that I'm angry at her, but I don't know which thing is supposed to be what makes me angry: that she waited to call for help, or that she called for help at all. I'm not upset about either, but she won't listen when I say as much. Her guilt gnaws at me, and all I can think about is her coming in and seeing me like that, how similar it must have been to the time that I found Dad just after he died.

I manage to stumble across the hall and into the shower, rinsing the blood from my pores. When I emerge, the sheets have been stripped from the bed, all of the bedding lying in a heap on the floor. Red-brown streaks wisp over the surface of the mattress.

Randy's perched on the bed, propped up on one elbow. He seems unbothered by the state of the mattress. As I enter the room, his gaze trails up from my pants to my bare chest—the ashy tone my bloodless complexion has taken, the livid bruises and lumps where ribs were rearranged. A wisp of hair grows along my breastbone, but otherwise the skin is smooth and bare and pale, a blank canvas for the evidence of death to paint itself against.

"Where's Zoe?" I rub a towel through my hair, let it fall over my shoulders.

"I sent her down to the corner store for some hydrogen peroxide," he says, rolling to his back and crossing his hands over his waist, staring disinterestedly at the ceiling. "Best thing for getting blood out of fabric."

" . . . In your car?"

"Of course."

"Jesus, Randy, she's sixteen. She can't drive by herself. She's barely got a learner's permit."

His head tilts, a partial shrug, but he doesn't move his gaze from the ceiling. "It's a few blocks. She'll be fine."

I think: *If she gets caught, if she gets pulled over, that's unwanted attention; that's trouble with the DMV; that's people prying into our affairs and finding God knows what to use against us.*

I also think: *When I was sixteen, I drove everywhere. I played DD for Dad. He'd tell me we were going somewhere fun and then leave me in the parking lot for hours while he drank with his buddies.*

"Anyway. I sent her out because I wanted to talk to you alone for a minute," Randy says, interrupting my thoughts.

That drags me back swiftly to the moment.

"Look. I get that you want a quiet life, Davin. I know you don't necessarily trust me, and I don't blame you for that. It's honestly pretty smart not to." He pushes himself up on his elbows, staring up at me now from my bald mattress. The gelled strands of pink hair fall back from his face; his turned-up chin throws the bruise on his neck into sharp relief. "But I promise, I'm not your biggest problem right now."

I avert my eyes, trying to avoid the intensity of his gaze.

"You don't have access to Lazarus," he continues, leaning forward, rolling onto his feet. He approaches me, leans in close enough that I can smell his aftershave. "I'm gonna guess you thought you had a plan, and it didn't work. But let me tell you something. You run out again, and you're goin' to cause a world of hurt for that little sister of yours. And I might not get here in time, next time."

He's right. Of course he is.

I imagine the people on the news, the Undead who tear at flesh and lunge, open-mouthed, at police and cameramen. I imagine grabbing for Zoe's body in my hands, fingertips curling into skin, bones snapping in my grip. I shudder violently, a sudden wave of nausea bubbling up from the tight depths of my ruined bowels.

What a selfish prick I am.

What if I'd woken up not myself? What if I'd lunged for her, attacked her, wrapped fistfuls of hair in my hands and bitten her like an animal?

For years, I'd kept Dad cooped up under lock and key, terrified of what he could do if he got loose, and I was fucking stupid enough to take the risk myself—because, what? I thought if I ignored this, if I pretended it wasn't happening, it'd somehow go away?

Randy takes my hand, fingers light against the skin. He shoves a piece of paper into my palm, curls my fingers around it. "There's a meeting in two days. Your sister paid for enough drugs to last you until then, but that's it. You think long and hard and decide whether you're with us or not. Decide whether you're ready to earn your keep."

My fingertips tighten around the paper, rolling it into a ball against my palm.

Outside my room, I hear the front door open, the sounds of Zoe entering. The rustle of a grocery bag.

"You keep saving me," I say while Randy's still close. "Why?"

He looks up at me, dark eyes catching mine, and it's like a curtain has lifted; their usual hooded, guarded quality has slipped, revealing something vulnerable beneath. "I guess because I know what it's like to die alone," he says, "and I don't want that for anyone. Not even a stranger."

He pushes past me, out into the hall, and when he speaks again it's in his usual lighthearted way, making banter with Zoe as they sort through whatever she brought home from the store.

Randy leaves, eventually. I notice, after he's gone, that our cabinets are filled with food I don't remember being there before: groceries for Zoe.

Late into the night, I'm awake, prowling the house. Zoe's asleep, and I'm glad that she's missing my restless pacing. It would probably frighten her. It's starting to frighten me.

The dryer buzzes, and I go to retrieve the sheets. There's a hint of discoloration, the ghost of a stain, but the bloody hues have gone. Good enough. Bundling them in my arms, I move back into my room to mechanically remake the bed.

I should turn myself in, I think. *Join my dad at the Lazarus House.* The idea strikes me out of nowhere, like a cartoon devil perched on my shoulder.

I abandon the bed, half-made, and go outside for a cigarette. It's dark and quiet out; no wind, no barking dogs in the distance. Just me, the glow of the cherry in the dark, and the loud echo of thoughts banging around in my head.

I'm thinking of the social worker and his quiet insistence that I didn't have to do what I was doing. That it could be so much easier just to let her go, to let someone else step in and help. What would he say if he knew I was here—a corpse, a ghost tethered to a body that has already begun to subtly decay? Somehow, I don't think he'd praise me for my valor.

But I can't give up.

She's sixteen. I know the kind of shit that happens to 16-year-olds in foster care. I can't do that to her. No matter what, I have to stay here for her.

I mull over Randy's words, again and again, and the address on the crumpled paper. *Decide whether you're ready to earn your keep.* I don't know what that means, or what Randy has in mind for me. But I know, whatever it is, that it's something I have to do.

I don't have any choices left.

"Can I come?"

"Absolutely not. It's not safe."

We've had this argument more times in the last 48 hours than I can count, and neither of us is showing signs of backing down. I'm sitting on the front porch bench, smoking a cigarette as I wait for Randy to arrive; Zoe's hovering, looking defiant. She's been coming at me like a snake, striking and retreating as if testing for weaknesses, the way she used to ask Mom and Dad for something separately, and play them against each other until she could get what she wanted—only now, there's no one to use as my foil. There's no one left to say, *Did you ask your mother?*

It's not stopping her from trying though.

"If Randy knows them, they can't be that bad."

"You hardly know him."

"But he's a good person." She crosses her arms, challenging me to argue that point. "He's saved you twice now. Twice!"

"I recall."

"And you still don't trust him? Jeez, Davin, talk about issues."

I put my head in my hand, rubbing at my temples. It's a reflex, a vestigial gesture. Before, when I was alive, my left eye would start to twitch under strain; the vein at my temple would pulse and throb. Now there's not enough blood oozing through my veins to make that happen, but some habits are ingrained deeper than the feelings that spawned them.

"It's not that I don't trust Randy," I say, measuring the words carefully. "It's that he is, by definition, a criminal. And that's inherently dangerous."

"If he is, then so are you."

She's right, and I take a long drag of my cigarette so I don't have to admit it right away. It's been a month now since I got the letter from the Lazarus House about Dad—just one month, and everything has tilted sideways.

A month ago, I thought I finally had the answer, that magic bullet solution that would remove the stress and heartache from my life and let us finally move on. A month ago, I thought sending Dad off to a facility was all it would take to be happy.

Now I'm dead, and I've got a whole separate set of problems to deal with.

The rest of the country's gone crazy, too. Each night, the news doubles down harder on its narrative about the dangerous Undead. Just a few weeks ago, you could have seen an Undead reading the newspaper at a bus stop or standing in line at the bank, Social Security check in hand; but now, there don't seem to be any Undead anywhere.

Anywhere, that is, but treatment centers. The Lazarus House is doing great business.

"Randy's here," Zoe says, interrupting my thoughts. Without waiting for me to reply, she bounds down the porch steps, meeting him in the driveway. Inviting herself along.

Before I have a chance to argue, she's installed herself in the back seat of the Mercedes. Reluctantly, I follow, folding myself once more into a passenger seat that's growing increasingly familiar.

CHAPTER ELEVEN

NEW MEXICO SPRAWLS. Even the small towns take up too much space, as if they'd been planned on a balloon before it was inflated. Everybody's got a yard that's too big to tend, a gravel driveway that ends up attracting old project cars and worn-out kids' toys, or else they live in little clustered neighborhoods and trailer parks that dot the landscape like islands. It's a little different in the cities. I spent a year in Albuquerque when I was still going to college, before Mom died, and there are places there that look like a real city. But if you drive far enough in any direction, even there, you find the sprawl, the empty lots and rural stretches. It's like a city that only pretends to be better than it is when somebody's watching.

Randy navigates his way through the streets of Los Ojos, and I stare at the town unfolding around us and try to get my thoughts in order enough to ask a question.

"So . . . where are we going?" Zoe beats me to it, leaning forward from the back seat, precariously balancing herself on the center console between us.

"Put your seatbelt on," I say automatically.

She glowers at me.

"He's got a point." Randy glances up in the rearview mirror. "I think the job of crash test dummy is already covered in your family."

Now it's my turn to glower, in part because of the jokey callousness of his words, but mostly because Zoe actually listens to him. I hear the click of the seatbelt as she slides back into place, feel a knee jab into the back of my seat as she squirms into a comfortable position.

"As for where we're headed..." Randy shifts across the lane to make a left turn without signaling, and my fingers claw into the leather padding on the door handle. "There's a meeting place for a few of us Undead. I want to introduce y'all."

"Why?" I blurt out the question, and I can practically feel Zoe's judgmental stare burning into the back of my seat. "I mean, is it some kind of . . . gang thing?"

Randy laughs. "If you want to call it that." He snickers, glancing at me sidelong, and then reaches for the center console to dig out a battered pack of smokes. He lights up two, handing me one without asking. "Look. Here's the deal. Every culture's got some figure who guides people into the underworld, right? Somebody has to show you the ropes on the other side. So think of me like your ferryman. Or *fairyman*, if you prefer."

He puts an affectation on "fairy," accentuated with a smirk. "But look, we're here. C'mon, kids, let's meet the family."

The meeting place, it turns out, is a coffee shop downtown. It's late evening by the time we arrive, and the streets are mostly quiet. Years back, this was a trendy neighborhood. Now it's mostly Section 8 housing and bus stops, with trash bag-wearing bums taking shelter beneath the benches. Everywhere are the bones of failed gentrification.

This is a part of town you're taught to avoid at this time of night; Los Ojos is small, but we have our share of villains, small-time gangsters and criminals working with the cartels. Parking on the street down here is an invitation to have your car stolen, but Randy doesn't seem to mind.

Then again, I suppose these days we *are* one of those things that goes bump in the night. Maybe that means I don't need to be so afraid, but tell that to my body. There's something trembling inside, deep down, as if all the places left empty in my gut have been filled with frightened birds.

The coffee shop appears to be closed. It's dark, with the overhead sign—old-school neon lights that read "CJ's" in outdated script—shut down. But the front door opens when Randy pushes it, and the three of us head inside.

CJ's is divided into two sections. The front area looks like any other shop: a chalkboard menu, a register, espresso machines, fridge. Round tables and larger booths cluster around the area. But if you push past them, there's a curtain that leads into a hall. On one end, the kitchen and, beside that, the bathrooms. Down the hall to the other side, a small back room with booths on either side. I imagine it's a cozy meeting place, or meant as a study space for high schoolers; there are electrical outlets above the tables, a lamp on each one. People have seated themselves around a booth, and the stark light of the lamp throws harsh shadows over their faces.

I recognize Ash and Lilith right away, and I turn toward them. But there's an older woman, maybe in her early 70s, who moves to intercept us. She's dressed like an old hippie, all flowing fabrics and dangling jewelry, and something about her feels familiar, although I'm certain I've never met her before. She introduces herself as Delilah and gestures for us to sit at the booth across the aisle from Ash and Lilith.

We take our seats, and I notice there are two other people here, both girls about my age. One is short and stocky, with blonde hair cut in a long bob and hints of a tattoo peeking out from beneath her sleeve. The other is—

"Holy shit. Jo?"

"Jesus, Davin! I had no idea you were . . . "

Faux-hawk. Short denim jacket over a cheetah-print mini-dress and black leggings. The glint of a stud at her left nostril.

How many months had I worked alongside her without realizing? "I didn't know you were, either."

"I'm . . . not." She looks down then, and I can see her cheeks flush with embarrassment. "This is my grandmother's shop. I guess you could call us . . . sympathizers?"

117

Randy leans back in his seat, looking amused. "You two know each other?"

I look from Jo up to Delilah, realizing suddenly why the older woman had seemed familiar. Now that I notice it, the resemblance is too striking to ignore.

Across the aisle, Jo's holding hands with the blonde girl. Their fingers entwine under the table.

"Yeah. We work . . . um. Worked together," I say. "How do *you* know each other?"

Jo tosses a look at Randy, questioning, apparently waiting for him to take the lead on answering.

"Anyway," Randy says loudly, clearly changing topics in a way that suggests he doesn't care he's doing it conspicuously. "Before we get going. Is there anyone left here who *doesn't* know my friends here?" He jabs a thumb in my direction. "That's Davin, our newest corpse. And this is his sister, Zoe. She's a Breather, but she's pretty all right. And you two"—he looks at us, then jerks his head over at the others—"that's Ash, Lilith, Jo, and Andrea."

There's some general murmur, low voices breaking off into a jumble of private conversation.

"All right then. I hope y'all fuckers have got my money, because I'm not runnin' a charity here. Oh! Delilah. Something for our fresh blood?" Randy glances at Zoe, brows lifted. "You drink coffee, right?"

Zoe nods as she folds herself up into the booth, actually managing to look shy. I've never known her to be shy a day in her life, but then, we've never had too many occasions to be in a crowd of strangers. We're not exactly socialites.

"Right. A coffee for the lady then. Something frou-frou, whipped cream and shit. And, uh . . . " He glances over at me. "You eating solid foods yet?"

I think back to the beans and rice incident, and firmly shake my head.

"Damn. All right. Make it black."

"I'm fine—"

"You know what, make it a double."

Delilah smirks and shuffles back into the kitchen to prepare our orders. I slide into place beside Zoe, nudging her closer to the wall. I'd like to pretend I'm not trying to shield her from the guys at the booth across the narrow aisle from us, but it's so obvious I wonder whether anyone is offended.

"So. Um." I look around at the group of them, these two couples and Randy, and feel supremely confused. "What . . . ?"

"We're the Underground," Jo says with a smile, as if this totally explains everything.

Apparently, for some of us, it does, because Zoe bolts upright beside me and flings an elbow into my side as she struggles to look past me. "Holy shit! Really?"

Everybody stares at us, or maybe just at her. It's a little hard to tell. I turn to look at her too, just as Randy slides into position across from us at our table.

"The Underground!" Zoe yelps excitedly, as if she just figured out that she was talking to her favorite band, which for all I know she could be. "I wasn't even sure you were a real thing. Like, I mean, I hoped you were, but . . . "

"Okay. Back it up." I can almost feel the pulse throbbing at my temple now, even though I don't really have a pulse there anymore. "I am *so* confused."

Zoe turns to look at me, and her faraway look is traded swiftly for exasperation. "Seriously, Davin? Don't you even watch my show?"

"I've been a little busy lately. Being dead and stuff." And also, no, I've never watched her show. I always kind of assumed she didn't want me to, like it would be super embarrassing. It's a boundaries thing. I figure nobody wants their stupid big brother slash father figure up in their 16-year-old business.

"Anyway. The Underground. They're this, like . . . Undead activist group. They're legendary. Grassroots. I guess there's groups of them all over the country, organizing protests and writing to lobbyists. So you guys are, what . . . the Los Ojos branch?"

I'm trying to wrap my head around the idea that Los Ojos, New Mexico, has enough people in it to form an activist group for anything, much less zombies, but Zoe's still yapping at me, tossing out various things that various branches of the group have done in various places.

"And you guys—" She's leaning forward now to talk past me, half her body sprawling over the table. Sugar packets spill onto the table as she knocks over the little basket that was holding them. "—are the ones who got Los Ojos PD to cough up the ashes of Ismael Gonzales so you could give him a funeral, right?"

"That was me," Ash says, blinking at us across the aisle. "Well. My lawyer, technically, but my idea."

I'm so lost. "Who is Ismael Gonzales?"

Zoe rolls her eyes. "Ismael Gonzales was the guy who was shot down by the cops earlier in the month. You know, *literally* right before they started to crack down on Undead living out of containment? Maybe the absolute *biggest* high-profile Undead shooting since this whole thing started?"

"Okay, okay. I get it. But . . . "

"Who *are* you?" Jo's girlfriend—Andrea—interrupts, looking at Zoe as if seeing her for the first time.

"UndeadLives," Zoe replies, remembering to look bashful again. "The YouTuber."

"Oh my God!" Jo squeals, in roughly that same tone of meeting a celebrity. "I totally watch your channel!"

"Well, I figured as much," Zoe says, looking suddenly bashful. "I mean, I hoped? It's so cool, though."

"I would never have guessed it was you! Oh my God, girl, your voice sounds so different online!"

"I run it through some distortion stuff, just enough to make it harder to identify. *Somebody_*is paranoid." Zoe jabs me again, on purpose this time, in the ribs.

I'm so lost. I cast a hopeless look around, trying to find someone who can clue me in on what's happening, but everybody's staring at Zoe. I get a sudden pang of regret that I haven't been following what she's been doing online more clearly.

Los Ojos has an activist group with at least five people in it. Zoe has enough YouTube followers that one of those five people has watched her channel.

There's a coffee shop with a secret Undead speakeasy gathering place.

What the fuck. What the actual fuck.

Zoe's still chattering. Something about a forum. Probably that deep web hidden wiki whatever-the-hell she's always talking about.

"So, which one of you is . . . Boner4U?"

Randy grimaces, but raises a hand. "I'm changing my name, though. It's CharonTheFairyman now. Try to keep up."

Delilah, thank God, shows up at that moment with coffee, and I try to take advantage of that break in conversation to grip the edge of the table and try to make sense of this sudden upheaval.

"Well, this works out great," Randy says, sliding out of his seat across from us. "See, here I was thinking you'd be bored, but turns out you're a local celebrity. I 'magine you got plenty to talk about now."

He maneuvers into the aisle and extends a hand, fingertips prodding into my shoulder. "You wanna join me out back for a smoke break while they catch up on the gossip?"

Maybe he noticed me going wall-eyed. But I'm grateful for the excuse to get out of here, and I follow him gratefully down the hall and out the employee exit.

Randy leans against the outer wall of CJ's, his skin especially pale against the brown adobe, and lights up a pair of cigarettes. He hands me one, and I take it, wondering at his odd habit of persistently lighting my smokes for me. But that's low on the list of questions I want to ask, so I just take a drag and stare at him and try to shove all of the unasked questions into a funnel so I can start asking them single-file.

"The Underground?" I manage, at least, and realize that's not even really a question.

He waves a hand dismissively, not meeting my eyes. His gaze travels across the narrow gravel lot behind the store, the dumpster that butts up against a fence and, beyond that, a squat laundromat whose burnt-out sign flickers and buzzes. "Feel-good hippie shit, mostly. But whatever makes folks feel better. It's nice not to be lonely, whoever your friends end up being."

He taps some ash off the end of his cigarette and shifts his weight, rotating his body closer to mine so he can look up into my face. There's something in his expression, some intensity, like he's preparing to say something big and has to gear up for it. I think: *This is it. This is whatever he actually brought me out here to tell me about.*

"So, that guy, Ismael Gonzales. You know anything about him?"

I shrug. "Just that he got shot. Drug-dealing, supposedly turned vicious, attacked some cops."

"Sure. Well, the part about him dealing Laz on the street, that was true. The rest of it, guess we'll never know, will we, seein' as his brains ended up all over the pavement. But Izzy had a job, and now there's a job opening. You follow?"

"You want me to run drugs for you."

"I want you to help me get Lazarus to folks who need it, so we don't end up seeing Zombie Apocalypse Now out on the streets."

I know, of course, that being an unregistered Undead is illegal. I know that the Undead need Lazarus, and if they're not getting it from doctors, they have to be getting it from somewhere. None of this is shocking to me. But the offer still hits me like a wall of ice.

"I mean, unless you want to go off Laz and try your luck."

I could turn myself in, I think. I could still drive down to the Lazarus House and check myself in and not have to worry about this. But that means Zoe goes into foster care. That means I'll probably never see her again, and God knows what will happen to her on her own.

But avoiding that means accepting a job previously held by a guy who got his brains blown out while doing the aforementioned job.

"Davin? You with me, buddy? Tell me what's going through your head right now."

The cigarette's burning down to ash in my fingers, unsmoked. I try to bring myself back to the present. I can't keep my eyes focused on anything; they're open, but all I'm seeing are my thoughts. "What if I get shot?"

"What if you do?" Randy stubs out his cigarette on the wall, adding to a line of dark circles, ghosts of cigarettes past. "You're already breaking the law just by existing, friend. When you measure the risks, it's not all that much more dangerous."

"Tell that to Izzy."

He frowns. "Yeah, well, Izzy had his own problems. Don't worry 'bout him. Look, I'll show you the ropes. And I'll pay you."

I look up at that, and hate myself for the hungry look I know is lighting up my face.

"Zoe mighta mentioned you lost your job."

"Goddammit."

Randy shrugs, digs into his pocket, and pulls out an envelope. He hands it over, and I ease open the flap, get a glimpse of a small stack of large bills. I frown.

"The hell is this?"

"Call it a cash advance, and an investment in the future. You need a car, last I checked, an' I sure as shit can't be driving mine all over town. Only thing more suspicious than the walking dead is a queer in a sports car."

I should argue. I should give him back the money. But I shove it greedily into my pocket instead, pushing it down deep and keeping my hand in there as if I'm afraid it's going to jump out and crawl away. I need the cash, and I hate that I need it. "So how . . . how does this work, exactly?"

Randy's looking me over, his signature smirk actually managing to reach his dark eyes for a change. He seems amused by my inexperience. "I'll fill you in on the details on your first job, assuming you take it. But the gist of it is, I've got a set of buyers. We keep tabs, best we can, on folks who might be recently shuffled off the mortal coil. Either they stay under the radar an' we sell to 'em, or they go above-board and get stuff they can sell to us. It's just a big circle, and all we're doing is closing up the gaps."

"That why you picked me up out on the highway?"

"Maybe that was part of it," he admits, and his smile freezes, eyes going dark. "Look. Sleep on it if you gotta, but I'll be at your house come morning an' we can get started if you're in. Now c'mon. Let's get inside 'fore your coffee gets cold."

I follow him back into CJ's, wondering what in the hell I've gotten myself into.

CHAPTER TWELVE

THAT NIGHT, AFTER Randy drops us off at home and Zoe bids me goodnight and disappears back into her room, I lie awake for a long time, just staring up at the ceiling. I realize I'm listening for the sounds of Dad moving around in his room across the hall, but of course he's not there.

I need to go see him, I think. *I need to take Zoe to visit. I need to see how he's doing.*

I wonder, now that I'm dead like him, if I can look him in the eye and forgive him for dying. I don't think I can. I might be a walking corpse now, but I'm still here and trying to make things work. That's more than I can say for him; he was dead for a long time before he finally stopped breathing.

After what feels like an eternity, I reach under my bed and pull out a dusty laptop; a piece of crap, honestly. It was a midline work machine when I was in college, and the intervening years haven't been kind to it. But Zoe's the one who cares about electronics and their specs and performance; I just need an old beater that'll navigate the internet the way my POS car used to navigate the roads.

It takes a while to boot up, and I shift uneasily in bed, shoving away blankets and sheets. It's desperately hot, despite the rattling of the air conditioner and the open window by my bed. I worry that I'll start sweating blood again, but it looks like sweating isn't really a thing I do anymore; that's got to be a zombie fever thing, a withdrawal symptom, because my body is stalwartly refusing to do anything to cool me off.

When I'm finally connected to the internet, I pull up my

browser and quirk a wry smile at the bookmarks: an even collection of job sites and porn. There was a time, not really so long ago, that I would have solved this bored insomnia with a few jerks and an old sock, but no part of that seems appealing anymore.

Can Undead even get it up, I wonder?

Necrophilia laws. Randy's voice jumps into my head unbidden, and I find myself imagining Ash, his colorless graying skin rubbing up against his wife's body, and if I was capable of having a boner before, I definitely am not anymore.

I click away from my bookmarks and go to YouTube. What was it Zoe said her channel was called? Right. UndeadLives.

She has more followers than I was expecting her to have, but I'm relieved that it's not an enormous number. A few thousand subscribers, and so, so many videos. I shouldn't be astonished at the number of them, considering how much of her life has been devoted to her research and her citizen journalism, but the list of them is daunting. I scroll through thumbnails of current-event news pieces and conspiracy theorist editorials with titles like:

Undead Shot Dead for Buying Household Cleaner
The Case for Legalizing Undead Marriage
Decriminalize the Undead!!!
Are There Any ACTUAL Confirmed Undead Rage Cases?
What's Actually In Lazarus? Pyadox Refuses to Say

I click on this last one, curiosity getting the best of me. The video takes a while to buffer, and when it finally starts, the sound is way too low; I have to back it up and start over after fumbling with the speaker settings.

The voice doesn't really sound like Zoe. I can recognize it, if I try, but she's done a good job of distorting it; I guess she must run it through some kind of sound filter or something. I feel a surge of pride at the care she's taken to protect herself—to protect us both. Thinking about that distracts me so much that I forget to pay attention to the first part of the video, and I have to back it up again to focus.

The video itself is just a series of slides, various generic images with voiceover. Images of pills, the Pyadox Pharmaceuticals logo, an old-fashioned syringe, some medical-themed stock photos—and then some bits of text pulled from what look to be scientific journals, with parts highlighted.

The voiceover is saying, "Lazarus. It's the miracle cure for the Undead—or is it? Let's look at the facts. Two years ago, drug company Pyadox introduced its life-extension drug. Lazarus was supposed to be the secret to helping Undead live among humans peacefully, but have we seen that happen? With the reports of Undead violence only increasing in number, it's clear that there are just a few explanations. Either Lazarus doesn't work the way they say it does, or the violence itself is being blown out of proportion to further some sort of political agenda. You look at the statistics and tell me what YOU think."

A chart pops up on the screen, detailing the various rates of Undead violence and attacks. They increase in a jagged slope, rising almost steadily since the outbreak began.

"So what's the deal with Lazarus? Is anybody asking how the fuck Pyadox just so happened to have a formula ready for the world population within six months of the first dead rising? Are we all just going to accept that they obviously cut some corners? Because if you're not scared yet, here's something that should make you worried: Nobody knows what's in Lazarus. Not really. If you visit the Pyadox Pharmaceuticals website, the ingredient list is notably missing. The formula has been redacted from all of the publicly available medical journals. There's protecting your proprietary formula, and then there's this."

More snippets of journals. More screenshots of the Pyadox website.

"So you tell me. What's Pyadox hiding? How does this drug work? *Does* this drug work? Drop your thoughts in the comments and until next time . . . keep asking the important questions."

The video reaches the end, and I stare at it a long time even as the next thing auto-plays. I barely notice; I can't concentrate. There's a thought nagging at the back of my mind, like something recently forgotten, but I can't get it into words.

Sleep won't come tonight. I resign myself to that, and settle in to watch the rest of the videos, my thoughts a muddle and tempestuous sea as the sky begins to brighten around the edges of the blackout curtains.

"So how did you get into this, anyway?"

We're in Randy's car, folded up uncomfortably into what's become an increasingly familiar position. He's gotten the worst of the gore cleaned out, but there are still dark stains on the upholstery, stubborn reminders of what's linking us together.

"Well, first I died . . . "

"Smartass."

He glances at me, smirking, and takes a moment to consider. "So we're unregistered, right? That's our whole deal. Half of that is taking your Lazarus and covering up your scars and learning how to pass for a Breather. The other half is dying without anybody knowing about it. You die in a hospital or get the ambulance called to pick up your corpse, and you get yourself a one-way ticket to the Undead Registration Office."

"Right."

"So, in my case, my father is . . . look, it's not important. The upshot is, I got shuffled off to New Mexico, where as far as anybody knows, I'm going to art school or some shit. He got his lawyer in contact with some other lawyer friend to keep an eye on me, and that guy knows Ash, so he hooked us up. Even the dead need friends, Davin. That's why they keep the graves so close together."

I try to follow the convoluted threads of this, but I think I get the gist of it.

"Anyway. Word gets around eventually, one way or another. Ash made friends with Delilah, she introduced us to Jo, Jo got us into the Underground, and all the while what I'm seeing loud and clear is that we need an organized Lazarus delivery system. You can't have a dozen different unregistered Undead walking around trying to buy their shit from different people. Too many points of failure, or however you wanna put it."

"So you stepped up to become the local zombie drug dealer out of the goodness of your heart."

"Something like that." He makes a turn, pulling off onto a county road that winds through a patch of empty desert lots and some spotty houses, big yards home to scruffy dogs and the yellow-flowering sprawl of puncture vine. "I might have known a thing or two about drug dealing from my past life. You never know when somethin' will turn out to be useful."

My eyes linger over his collar, which at the moment is pulled up tight around his throat, concealing the purple rope burn there. He's wearing makeup too, dark eyeliner that makes his pale skin look like a fashion choice instead of a side effect of his death. I wish I'd thought to do the same. "Okay. So what is it you need me for?"

He pulls up to a gate of some property, a double-wide trailer sitting up on blocks visible at the end of the gravel drive. There's a big dog, something red-brown and fuzzy, standing behind the gate with its shaggy tail wagging in slow, methodical swipes. He doesn't look especially friendly.

"So today, I'm just showing you the ropes. Once you get your car situation worked out, you'll be doing deliveries and pickups. I'll handle the social stuff. You don't strike me as the type."

Randy lays on the horn, muttering something about somebody needing to come tend to this damn dog, and I'm feeling more than a little out of my depth, but I keep quiet and repeat the constant mantra that's been keeping me going so far: Zoe needs me, and I need Lazarus, and if this is what I need to do then it's what I'm going to do.

It does a fairly inadequate job of quieting the other chant, that incessant hammering of anxiety at the back of my mind that's demanding: What if I get caught? What if I can't trust Randy? What if I've already blown my cover? What if this is all some elaborate setup? What if, what if, what if. The beat of my uncertainty is heavier and more rhythmic than my stuttering pulse.

A lady comes down the path, making some vague gesture to the dog, who bounds in a circle around her and makes big, booming "woofs" that are only somewhat muffled by the windows of the Mercedes. The lady goes to the gate, fumbling with a lock, and then gestures for us to come on. Randy hesitates a moment, then eases open his door, and I follow suit, glancing around at the sleepy county road as if expecting a cop or a CDC van to come rolling by any second. But the road is quiet, and I trail Randy to the gate.

"Who's this?" The lady squints at me, suspicious. She's middle-aged, her hair patchwork shades of brown in a way that suggests she's been dyeing it badly at home for a long time. There's something familiar about her, but I can't quite place it.

"Buddy of mine. Don't you worry 'bout it, he's all right." Randy flashes a smile.

She relents and shoves the gate open; it rattles as the gap widens just enough for the two of us to squeeze in. The dog is on me immediately, his wide head and boxy muzzle smashing into my abdomen, making me grimace as he sniffs enthusiastically at my sewed-up wounds and bruised, smashed-in ribs.

Undead-sniffing dogs, I think, and a thrill of panic rolls through me.

But Randy doesn't pay it any mind, and he's up ahead, chatting amiably with the lady like everything's normal. I try to play it cool. I extend a hand for the dog to sniff, letting his cold nose bump against the back of my knuckles, feeling the warm rasp of a tongue crossing my room-temp flesh. I imagine him closing his mouth over my hand, tearing it off; a sudden vivid image of chasing him for the chewed-up remnants, a stump oozing black blood.

But it doesn't happen, and I suck in a lungful of air, reminding myself to breathe. The inhalation rattles through my chest, and the dog's fuzzy triangular ears prick forward in curiosity at the sound.

The lady opens the door to the trailer, and we climb inside single-file, dog and all. There's somebody sitting in a battered La-

Z-Boy in the living room, pointed vaguely in the direction of a mammoth box-style TV, the grainy picture playing a telenovela with the colors skewed, casting everyone in a greenish hue.

He turns to face us as we enter, and I realize, with a sickening swoop in my gut, who he is—why the lady looks so familiar.

I don't know his name, but you never forget a face like that. What's left of it, anyway: the ragged meat of torn-up flesh and the empty socket where a nose had been, the drooping unseated eyeball. The guy who tried and failed to kill himself a second time, who I used to share an awkward waiting room with so many times when Dad was getting his monthly Lazarus certifications.

The lady—this guy's daughter, I think, or maybe once his wife, it's hard to tell how old he is with most of his face missing— says something I don't quite hear and excuses herself down the hallway.

Randy leans in close, standing on his toes to whisper in my ear. "She's a little twitchy. I'm going to go talk to her. Make yourself comfortable."

He spares me a lopsided grin laced with irony, claps me on the back, and vanishes down the hallway.

It's just me and the guy with no face, and I stand awkwardly, not sure on the protocol here. Do I sit down? Do I try to strike up conversation? The Undead seems to be staring at me, but it's honestly hard to tell with his drooping eye trailing down his bandaged cheek.

He doesn't say anything, but he lifts a hand and motions toward the couch, and I hesitantly tread past him and settle onto the edge of the cushion, quelling the urge to fidget. I can't quite keep myself still though, and I start rhythmically popping the joints of each finger, over and over until I'm half afraid the bones will snap.

The dog, still apparently fascinated by me, jumps up onto the couch beside me and shoves his big shaggy head into my side, thrusting his face under my hand. I bury my fingers in his fur, grateful for the distraction.

The guy with no face makes a throaty, strangled noise that sounds like choking. I glance at him and see his body shuddering, minuscule convulsions that tremor through his frame. I realize that he's laughing.

"Your dog is nice," I offer as a point of conversation.

He grunts and swallows noisily, like battling back a retch.

I only dimly remember my grandfather—he died when I was little, leaving most of my memory-making to my grandma—but this faceless Undead reminds me of him in some way. My grandfather didn't speak English, and we'd learned to communicate through a similar language of grunts and gestures and shared silence. I remember he'd take me onto his knee and give me strange sweets, candies laced with mango and chile powder, and sometimes he'd stuff dollar bills into my pocket with a conspiratorial wink.

The memory warms me toward this guy, this stranger who shares so much with me but who's impossible to know. I give up on trying to communicate and turn instead to the television, letting myself get engrossed in the grainy melodrama, the rhythmic motion of fingers raking through fur, the hot breath of a dog snuffling against my body.

It's not home, but it feels like it almost could be, and it's the most comforting thing I've experienced since I woke up dead in a ditch off the interstate. I cling to this, because I know it can't possibly last.

Randy emerges back into the front room eventually, and nods for me to follow him outside. I spare an awkward smile and half-wave at the Undead and the woman, who's still watching me suspiciously. The dog follows us out to the gate.

"Here." Randy thrusts a package into my hand. Wrapped in a brown paper bag, it appears to be a margarine container. I try to peek inside, but he makes a vague gesture at me to stop and I look at him instead, questioning. "One down."

"He's not unregistered," I say, feeling stupid. Randy fumbles with the gate latch, and I pat the dog and make a gesture I hope it understands means "stay." It leans against my leg instead. "I know him."

"Obviously he's not unregistered," Randy says, exhaling a slow breath of impatience. He gets the gate open and I squeeze through, leaving the dog to stare at me from the other side of the chain link. "We're buying, not selling."

I lift my brows.

"Oh, for fuck's sake. Get in the car." Once we're both inside, he shakes his head and glances into the mirror, adjusting the edge of his eyeliner with a pinkie finger. "Okay, so it's like this. Doctors prescribe Lazarus at a daily dose, right?"

"Right." I remember Dad's nightly injections, the monthly recertification, the regular pharmacy visits and pre-marked syringes.

"So you don't need Laz every day. Maybe you skip a couple days a week. Usually you can go three, four days without hitting any withdrawal symptoms. Somebody like our pal Roberto in there, who's been on the drug for years, can last a little longer. It builds up, right? So I come along, and I make folks an offer. You skim some meds, set 'em aside for me, I roll through and pick up your extras every so often."

"That's it? That's how you get enough Lazarus for all your buyers?"

He shrugs. "It's part of it. There's some other ways, too. Sometimes folks can get a script filled a couple times at a couple of different pharmacies. Sometimes somebody gets hold of a doctor's Rx pad and has a good time. Once in a while an Undead goes and gets himself double-dead somehow, and I buy up the family's excess. I had a buddy for a while working at the hospital, but he lost his job and snip-snip." He makes a scissor gesture with his fingers.

"Isn't it dangerous? Aren't you worried people will start to turn if they're not getting enough?"

He shrugs. "If they do, I've never seen it happen. For all I

133

know, the whole thing's a myth. But you get real sick before anything else can happen. You know that. Most folks who go to the doctor aren't gonna get far enough into that nasty withdrawal to see what's on the other side of it. It's just us out on our own who have to worry about running out for good."

"Do we?" I ask.

"What?"

"Do we have to worry about that?"

His grip tightens on the steering wheel. "Not yet."

But I'm starting to wonder. With more Undead getting sent to the Lazarus House, how long will it be until we're the only corpses left on the streets?

We end up back at CJ's. Randy stopped along the way to pick me up a prepaid phone, and I spent most of the car ride fumbling with packaging and trying to figure out how to make the thing work. I barely notice that we've come to a stop when he puts the car in gear and turns toward me.

"Mess with that later," he says. "Or just hand it to your sister when you get home. She seems like the type."

I hate that he's right. I tuck the phone and a mess of extra plastic into the center console and look up at the flickering CJ's sign. "What are we doing here?"

"Getting you on payroll."

I blink at him, not getting it, and he heaves a long-suffering sigh.

"The money for Lazarus gets laundered through the coffee shop," he explains, starting to get out of the car and waiting for me to catch up. "We're still supposed to be alive, Davin, or did you forget? Death and taxes. We can cheat the one, as it turns out, but not the other."

"But you paid me."

"To get you started. Which, by the way, you'd better hurry up on that car situation. Now c'mon. I want to snag a dark roast while we're here."

We head inside. The coffee shop isn't much more crowded during business hours than it was when it was closed. We start toward the counter, but I see Randy tense up ahead of me just as a voice comes up from a table near the door: "Eyyy, white boy!"

I look over at the source, two guys who look decidedly out of place at a coffee shop. One's wearing a faded blue-checkered flannel shirt open over a white wifebeater, three blue dots tattooed in a triangle under his right eye. The other is wearing a Raiders jersey and a bandana tied over his brow; I can't make out the pattern of his full-sleeve tattoo from here, but the tendrils of ink crossing over his skin are fading out from age.

Randy grimaces, but makes his way over to them. They don't make a move to rise from their chairs; bandana guy leans back, legs and arms in a wide and inviting stance, the kind of cool guy who has to prove how much he doesn't care. I follow behind Randy, looking between the two, silent. Flannel shirt looks familiar. I wonder if I might have gone to high school with him.

"You got the shit, or what?"

Randy shoots him a look that suggests he's both irritated and disgusted. "It's in the works." He glances over his shoulder, scanning the room; we seem to be pretty much alone, as far as prying ears go. "But, much like your sense of subtlety, it ain't here yet."

"Who's this?" Bandana tilts his head, thrusting his chin questioningly in my direction. "Your new runner?"

"Yeah, man, sorry what happened to Izzy. That guy was aight."

I glance at Randy, not sure if giving a name here would be appropriate, but Randy doesn't meet my gaze so I stay quiet, suddenly particularly aware of the height difference between us as I loom behind him.

"I'm sure he'd be touched," Randy says dryly, and starts to take a step back. "Y'all be sure you're paid up, an' I'll get to you when I can. Usual place."

"You better," flannel shirt says. "We start to go loco, I promise it's your house we find first, you feel?"

"Looking forward to it," Randy mutters, and turns, nudging me away.

I can feel the eyes of the others on my back, but they don't say anything else. "The fuck?" I ask quietly, when we've pushed through the curtains to the back room, safely out of earshot.

"That would be the Martinez brothers."

I shoot him a questioning look.

"Everybody dies," Randy says, shrugging. "Gang-bangers included, I guess." His brow furrows. "Though, to tell you the truth, I'm not entirely sure they're even dead."

"Seriously?"

"I mean they pass real well, is all. Haven't seen a mark on 'em. For all I know, they've got a cousin someplace they're trading it to for meth." He pauses, frowning, and looks up at me. Amusement glitters in his dark eyes. "Was that racist?"

I ignore him. "Does that happen? People trading Lazarus for drugs?"

He shrugs. "Black markets are funny like that. Anyway— come on. We've got places to be, right? Oy! Delilah!"

He makes his way into a small office tucked away beneath an "Employees Only" sign, and Delilah smiles her welcoming old-lady smile and gestures me in. Within minutes, she's got me on payroll, and is explaining the way the system works. I have to admit, it's pretty clever the way they've got everything set up.

Undead stop off at CJ's and place an order for a specialty drink that's not on the menu. Delilah takes their money and writes a time and place on the receipt. Jo comes in on the weekends to fix the books and make the numbers work out, and Randy and I go on payroll as full-time employees, getting the money that's shuffled around through the business, paying taxes like upstanding citizens.

"That way nobody's carrying cash when you go to make a delivery," Randy explains. "Seemed safer that way."

My job, he tells me, is to show up at the pre-appointed time to drop off the goods and take back the receipt—proof of payment. That all seems easy enough, and just like that, I'm fully inducted into my new life of crime.

CHAPTER THIRTEEN

LOS OJOS DOESN'T exactly have the infrastructure for public transportation, but there is one lonely bus route that makes a sprawling loop of the town. Two, if you count the shuttle from here to the casino, delivering the occasional wayward and bored tourist who's picked up a hotel here for the night on their way to something better.

But I'm on the other bus, the one that snakes its way over the main roads in the least efficient path possible. Getting on it means walking two miles to the bus stop at Wal-Mart and waiting 45 minutes for a bus to come by, looking as casual as possible while surrounded by other hollow-faced commuters: the bag ladies with their canvas sacks that smell vaguely like cat urine; the drunks who ride past all the stops, using it as a climate-controlled place to sleep it off until they can go home; the wage slaves who wake up two hours early to ride to their fast-food jobs because they can't afford the cars or the insurance or the gas to get to work any other way.

Sitting here on the hard plastic seat, I can't help but wonder how many of the people around me are dead.

Ever since Randy opened my eyes to the possibility of an Undead underworld, of people shuffling through life working and getting by and spending their wages on bootleg Lazarus, everyone's suddenly suspect. The leathery skin and soul-dead dark eyes of my fellow commuters could be the side effect of death, or the result of a life that's gone on too long under too-hard conditions—it's impossible to tell.

Sometimes it's easier. There was a guy a few stops back who

tried to climb aboard, who was missing most of his face. There were maggots crawling in the red-black goo where his eyeball should be. The bus driver wouldn't let him aboard, citing some kind of health code regulation that might have been thought up on the spot. It's getting hard to tell the difference between the laws regulating Undead behavior and pure bullshit made up on the spot by people too afraid to share space with reanimated corpses.

I've been riding for close to an hour and a half, getting to an address that should be a 20-minute drive from my house. But if things go well, this is the last time I'll have to do it.

The money's burning a hole in my pocket. I keep touching my wallet through my jeans pocket, afraid that it might have slipped out somehow. I've got $2,000 in cash, crisp hundred-dollar bills courtesy of Randy, and it's the most money I've ever had at one time. The truck I found on Craigslist was listed at $1,700, so I'm hoping I can walk away from this with some extra to pay the utilities and buy Zoe some food and put some kind of shitty insurance on it so I'm street-legal.

It's nice, worrying about dumb shit like this again. It feels normal, in a way that nothing else has felt normal since that night on the bridge.

I haven't told Randy or Zoe or anyone else about what I saw up there. I'm half-convinced that I made it up, that I was seeing things. I can't trust my memory so close to my death.

Outside, the skies have darkened, threatening afternoon rain. I try to pretend that it doesn't make me uneasy. Driving a pickup home in the rain from one side of a shitty town to the other shouldn't be frightening. What's the worst that can happen, right? I'm already dead.

The bus rolls to a stop at a light, one of the busier intersections in town. There's a guy standing on the corner, holding up a cardboard sign with words spelled out in careful block letters: *REPENT. The end times have come.* He spies me watching through the bus window, meets my eyes across the distance and the glass. He flips over his sign. It reads: *Hell is full. All the devils are here.*

The light changes, and the bus jerks back to life. I look away, breaking eye contact, staring down at my lap. Something shifts and twists uncomfortably in my guts; I'm afraid for a moment that I might throw up, spewing the black tar of my ruined innards all over the floor; that they'll throw me out on the curb or call Undead Services to haul me away.

But the urge passes, and I sit up shakily, realizing I've arrived at my destination.

The truck is a piece of shit, but I was expecting that.

It'd be weird, honestly, to drive anything else. Besides, I figure part of what Randy's paying me for is fitting in. He draws too much attention to himself simply by existing. If we're trying to go incognito, this truck is the right kind of camouflage.

It's beat up, one of those old silver Toyotas that seems like it's already survived through an apocalypse or two. But it runs well enough, and—unlike my last car—it comes with a clean title and working airbags.

I'm moving up in the world.

The seller, though, is an asshole. Not on purpose, I don't think. Just one of those people you don't want to be stuck talking to, the kind of guy who's used to saying whatever comes into his head and assuming that anybody who's listening to him has got to be on his side.

I'm pretty much trapped here until he hands me the keys, seeing as the bus won't be back around for over an hour. I'm here to buy this truck, however much of a lemon it may or may not be, and he knows it just as well as I do. You don't show up to buy a car on foot and expect to haggle.

"So, where you from, kid?"

He's insisting on making small talk, even though I'm ready to just give him his money and get out of here. I guess maybe he's lonely. He's middle-aged in that soft way, all rounded edges and doughy skin, the way that suggests he's had a comfortable life, maybe a little too comfortable. The car, he's told me, was his son's starter vehicle, ready to be discarded now that he's gone off to college in something newer, shinier. Lucky him. The guy— he's told me his name, but I let it slip right past my memory, imagining I'd never need to know it—made a big thing about what a spoiled brat his kid is, what a waste of money the school is, how his wife was coddling the boy, how in his day what mattered was somebody's character and the work they put in. The monologue stinks of humble-bragging.

"Here," I tell him.

"Originally?"

"Born and raised." *And dead and risen*, I think, but don't add. Maybe one of these days, if I die, the Underground will pay for a funeral for me the way they did for Izzy. Then I could say I was buried in the same town I was born in, the shameful achievement anyone growing up in Los Ojos hopes to avoid.

"That's good," the guy says, but he looks distracted. I feel his eyes crawling over my skin, trailing the hastily-sewn scar along my cheek. It's not healing, exactly, but the skin has sort of melded back together, like the edges of pressed dough. "You know what it's like then. Having it rough. That's good. Builds character."

I arrange my face into what I hope is a polite smile, and he pries open the door to dig around in the glove box for the title.

"You sure you don't want to drive it a little more? Take it out on the highway?"

"It's fine," I reply, still trying for the blandest smile possible. I can only imagine why he's so keen to keep me here talking, to go joyriding with a stranger. Maybe he's trying to stay away from some henpecking wife. Maybe selling a car is the most interesting thing he'll do all month, and he wants to make the moment last. "I'm sure you've got places to be too."

He waves his hand, a dismissive gesture, silently continuing his search through the glove box. He pulls out a mess of papers and starts to paw through them. "You know how to write a bill of sale?"

"What?"

"The bill of sale. You need that for the DMV, right?"

"I think you can just . . . write something," I offer, hazily, honestly not remembering how it worked the last time I bought a car. My last car came from a police auction. Which, come to think of it, is probably where it ended up again—as scrap metal this time, assuming anyone bothered to fish it out of the river bed. "It doesn't have to be anything fancy."

"Right. Sure. What'd you say your name was?"

"Davin Montoya." I hesitate, then go ahead and spell it out for him before he has a chance to ask.

His brow furrows over it; then he looks back at me. "Montoya. That a Mexican name?" Now I know he's fucking with me, because nobody's lived in New Mexico long without knowing at least three people with the name Montoya. "Davin, though. That's a funny name for your kind of people."

I can't help but bait him a little. "It's Hebrew."

"Hebrew. No shit." He looks down at the paper where he was writing out, presumably, a bill of sale, then looks back up at me, clearly baffled. "You some kind of Jew?"

"Something like that."

"I'll be damned. A Mexican Jew. You learn something new every day." He folds up the paper and hands it over to me with the keys, palm extended for the money. I wait for him to make a comment about it, something appropriately off-color about counting it. I can see it lighting up in his eyes, the way a dog's eyes change just before it bites, but I guess he thinks better of it, because his mouth snaps shut before it leaks out.

I hand him his money and take the keys and, finally, am able to get out of there. I pull out of the parking lot with something like regret.

It's almost nice, somehow, running into some casual racism that isn't tied up in being a corpse. It rounds out the day, really: worrying about money, buying a shit car from a chatty white guy, riding the bus. It's the most normal I've felt since this whole thing started, and it's comforting in its familiarity. If I don't think too hard on it, if I don't remind myself where the money came from and what I've promised to do because of it, I can pretend that everything is normal.

Until I forget to make myself breathe, anyway. Until that tingle of Lazarus withdrawal reminds me of what I am, and what's at stake if I let myself forget too long.

Zoe is angry when I get home.

I can hear her yelling—what she might call having a passionate conversation—beyond the door before I even cross the threshold of the porch. Her tone suggests that she's talking to someone she finds very stupid, and is about to roast them.

I pause, hand on the doorknob, to listen.

"—the fuck do you mean, minor-restricted access? They're Undead, for fuck's sake, not pedophiles." A breathless pause, a sharp intake of air. "I'll use whatever kind of language I want, you inbred bureaucratic shoe-licking— Hello? Son of a whore!"

I open the door.

Zoe's wearing pajama bottoms and an old, faded t-shirt that I think might have once belonged to Dad. She's pacing angrily between the kitchen and living room, bare feet padding a well-worn path alongside the table. Her phone is clenched so tightly in her hand that I'm afraid she might break it.

"Um."

She doesn't notice me at first. She mutters something profane, slamming her phone down on the counter and yanking her glasses off to clean them, aggressively rubbing the lens on her shirt hem.

"What was that about?" I try again, standing in the door frame. I'm prepared to duck back outside of it in case she decides to throw something at me, but she looks like she's already calming down. The passion is fading to something more like a cold fury.

"Was just on the phone with those motherfuckers at the Lazarus House," she says, putting her glasses back on and then immediately taking them back off to clean them again. "Guess who changed their policy about visitation."

That is, obviously, a rhetorical question, so I stay quiet to let her get it all out. It's wise not to interrupt Zoe when she's on a roll.

"So now, not only can I not see Dad, I can't even step foot on their goddamn premises. It's *bullshit*. There's no reason for it. They let kids into fucking prisons, Davin. *Prisons*. If Dad was an axe-wielding psychopath, great! I could waltz right in and see him! But no, he's just *dead*, so now I can't."

I'm reasonably sure that's not quite how prisons work but, again, I stay quiet. It looks like she's winding down. She puts her glasses back on and shoves them up the bridge of her nose, finally looking at me.

"It doesn't make any sense. It's the stupidest thing I've ever heard of in my life. What are they worried about? All the Undead are going to corrupt the youth somehow? We're going to see them and be like, 'Ooh, being dead sure sounds fun! I guess I'll go die now!' I mean, seriously, fucking *what*. What is their deal?"

The look Zoe sends me now is plaintive. The anger has mostly seeped out of her, and she's looking vulnerable and small, younger than her 16 years. With her pajamas and untidy hair, she looks like a child, a little kid woken up on her birthday to find the party's been canceled.

She's expecting some sort of answer, but I don't have one for her, so I just shrug. "I'll go talk to them," I say, knowing it probably won't make any difference. "You're right. It's BS. I'm sorry."

Her nose wrinkles.

"Did . . . if you want me to tell him anything. In particular." I'm about to offer to deliver a message, but I choke on it. Because I can't imagine my mouth forming to make words for the kind of things she might want to say to him, not if I have to look him in the face to do it. "Maybe they'll let him use the phone. I'll talk to him. We'll figure it out."

That gets her to smile a little, and she leans over to peer past

me now, looking at the gaps between me and the door frame.
"Did you get it?"

"The truck? Hell yeah, I did." I grin and step sideways so she
can see. "Go get dressed and we'll take a ride."

"Can I drive?"

"I just bought the damn thing!" I affect a voice of mock
indignation and outrage to cover up the actual feelings of
indignation and outrage. "Let me get insurance on it first."

"You know, statistically, you've wrecked more cars than I
have."

"Statistically, you're a pain in my ass." She grins at me, and I
grin back. "Now go get dressed. We can go to CJ's, maybe. Swing
by Randy's place. I'm sure he wants to see . . . " *What his money
bought.* I catch myself before this last bit comes out.

But it doesn't matter, because Randy's name is like a magic
word, and she's already bounding down the hall for a shower
and a change of clothes.

I wonder whether I'll ever get to be the cool one again. With
Randy as my competition, it doesn't seem likely.

CHAPTER FOURTEEN

THE LAZARUS HOUSE seems emptier now than when I visited the first time. I go through the security at the gate and wait at the front desk to be led out to visit Dad in his quarters. It's not Chuy who takes me; some other guy, less chatty and with a stormier expression, meets me in the admin trailer and leads me through the courtyard to the block of rooms on the other side.

There's no one outside today. The cement tables are empty. No one is out shuffling around on the dying grass and dirt, play-acting at normalcy. I think about asking why, or asking about Chuy, but the look on the orderly's face dissuades me. It's somewhere between an "I hate my job" face and a "don't fuck with me" face, and I fall in step behind him.

There are no faces staring out at me from doorways, no curious tragic children gazing out of bloated, drowned faces. Only the sound of our shoes scuffing the dirt, and birds overhead, roosting in the eaves and overhangs of the old building.

"Here you go," the orderly says, pulling keys from a heavy key ring on his pocket, flipping through them until he finds the right one. "I'll give you half an hour. I'll be just outside if you need anything." He hesitates, then adds, "Good luck."

I think that sounds unnecessarily foreboding, but I head inside all the same, bracing myself for whatever's on the other side.

The room is Spartan: a metal cot and thin mattress, a metal folding chair. It looks like the inside of a prison cell. Adobe is flaking off the walls, forming broad cracks; a cockroach is nestled in one, its antennae poking out from the darkness.

Dad's sitting up in bed, hugging his knees to his chest. He looks up at me when I enter, and I get a sudden, painful pang of déjà vu.

"Hey, Dad."

His eyes roll up to me. Lucid, clear. A little sad. I almost wish they were far away instead. Never in my life have I wanted to open the door to see his glassy-eyed stare, the distant look of someone living in his own head, but right now I'd give anything for that as an alternative. The lucidity is killing me.

"I didn't know you were coming."

"Yeah, well, I just figured I'd drop in." The words sound lame, ringing false. I move to sit in the folding chair, turning it around to straddle it so I can rest my chin on the back. "Zoe wanted to come, but they won't let her. I'm going to try to get them to let you schedule a phone call."

"She's a good kid. Always cared about her old man."

I can't help but hear a scathing condemnation in those words, and don't want to rise to them. I didn't come here to start a fight. Silence settles between us, him watching me with cold dark eyes and me trying hard to avoid them.

When it's clear that he's not going to keep talking, I try again to start conversation. "So. Uh. How have you been? Are you . . . doing okay?"

He fixes me in a cool stare. He's more lucid today than I've seen him in a long time, certainly since his death. He looks sober, and I don't even know how that's possible.

"You left me here," he says finally. "Like a dog you didn't want anymore."

"Sometimes dogs are happier in new homes," I say, and

146

immediately grimace that I'm continuing this metaphor. I don't know what it says about me that I don't immediately reach for some other way to explain; I don't know what it means that my father comparing himself to a dog doesn't seem all that far off. "At least I didn't put you down."

He gives a rare smile. I don't expect it, and the expression takes me by surprise, knocks me off-center. It's like looking in the mirror: his smile looks just like mine.

"You'll never let that go, will you?" he asks.

When I was a kid, we had a dog, the only pet we ever kept. We were usually too busy for animals, or else Dad didn't want the extra responsibility. But this dog was, for a little while, a part of the family.

It was a Springer Spaniel my dad picked up from some corner, a guy with a pickup truck and a box of puppies. I guess he'd been feeling charitable that day, struck by some rare bit of sentimentality. She was a sweet, dumb thing, poorly-bred and clumsy. I don't even remember her name anymore, but I'd loved her at the time. She was my constant companion, like a sibling before Zoe was born. We did everything together.

Until, one day, she snapped, as if something had broken in her mind. We'd been all alone together, me and the dog and my father—before things got bad in his head, back when the problems were contained to just a vacant sort of depression, bouts of misery that were subtle enough for a child to miss entirely.

The dog was playing with us, chasing sticks, and then suddenly she looked at me and her head tilted and something seemed to die behind her brown eyes. Then she lunged at me, teeth bared, as if planning to tear off my face.

My dad caught her before she could get far, grabbing her by the throat and around the waist and holding her still. He was fearless back then, and he wrapped his calloused fingers around her snout and carried her to the car, and we kept her in the trunk in case she went vicious again. We drove her to the vet, and Dad tried to get me to wait outside, but I insisted on being indoors.

"It's just a thing that happens sometimes with these dogs," the vet had said, looking her over. She was wearing a muzzle now, but the brokenness behind her eyes had faded, and she looked as scared and dumb as ever. "We call it sudden onset aggression. It's like a type of seizure. They don't even know what they're doing. But once it happens, it can recur any time."

"And there's no way to stop it?" my father had asked, mostly for my sake. I'm pretty sure he didn't give a shit about a dog, not even back then.

The veterinarian shook his head, and my father gave him the go-ahead, and they held her down when they gave her the injection that would stop her heart.

I had almost forgotten about the dog, but now that Dad's mentioned it, it's like she's here in the room—a ghostly spaniel, fixing us with a judgmental stare from the corner.

Without warning, I'm thinking about Izzy, my predecessor: his body flattened to the pavement, blood and gore oozing from his ruined skull. I'm thinking about all that news footage of Undead losing themselves, going feral, needing to be rounded up and put down.

Maybe that's all we are, I think, and can barely contain the shudder that runs through me. *Maybe we're all just mad dogs that deserve to be put down.*

"You never believed me," Dad's saying, and his voice brings me back to the present. "But I loved that fucking dog."

"No you didn't. You hate dogs." His words take me by surprise, yet another shock in what's turning out to be a day full of the unexpected. "We never had another one."

"Would *you* have gotten another dog?" His voice is incredulous. "If your dog went crazy, almost attacked your kid, and you had to hold her while they killed her—would you risk ever doing that again?"

I stare at Dad, meeting his eyes. I'm floored. I don't know what to say. I don't even know if we're still really talking about the dog anymore. I wasn't expecting any of this.

Outside, there's the sounds of conversation. I can't make out the words, but there's the mumble of voices, a bark of laughter. It's an incongruous sound here; there's never been a room that looks so humorless.

"There's something changed about you, *mijo*," he says, after silence has settled between us. "Something different."

I freeze.

My first impulse is to tell him—to divulge this terrible secret that now defines my existence. I want to tell him, *Dad, I finally understand. I know what you're going through now.* So many things I never understood before are thrown into sharp relief now that I've crossed over, become a member of that most exclusive club that no one wants to join.

But I can't tell him. Because he's in here, and I'm not. Because he'd give me away out of spite.

"I'm not angry, if that's why you're here," Dad says. There's no malice in his words; if anything, he just sounds tired, weary. "Inside one room, inside another, there's no difference to me."

"I didn't know what else to do," I mutter.

"I know."

I don't dare to lift my eyes; I can feel his gaze on me, and I feel like I might burn beneath it. Before I can say anything, before I can sort out how I feel about this conversation that's gone so surprisingly sideways, the door opens.

"Mr. Montoya. Sorry to interrupt." It's Chuy, looking as massive and cheerful as ever. He sees me, and flashes a smile that almost covers for the surprise in his eyes. "It's time for your meds."

"Okay." Dad shifts his weight, scooting to the edge of the bed and rolling up the sleeve of his shirt.

Are you fucking kidding me, I think. I can't keep the incredulity from my face; it hangs there almost like disgust. For two years, I fought nightly with Dad over the injections. For two years, I had to deal with his huddling anxious and paranoid in the corner, lashing out at me like a frightened animal, or else railing at me, screaming obscenities. But here he is, gentle as a lamb, bright-eyed and even smiling a little.

Something in me burns, deep down. I'm not sure if it's jealousy or resentment, or where one ends and feeds into the other.

But the injection is administered in the blink of an eye, faster than it takes me to process what I'm feeling, faster than it takes for me to get my jaw back in place and wipe the shock from my face, and then Chuy and Dad are making small-talk, some doctor-patient in-joke that feels designed to exclude me.

Maybe Chuy catches the look in my eye, but he turns to me and cracks a broad smile. "Davin, hey. It's good to see you."

"Yeah," I reply back, feeling hollow. I've just about forgotten what I came here for, what any of this is about. In the back of my mind I'm wondering, *Holy shit. What if Dad's actually getting better somehow? What if they're actually treating them here?* Overlaying this, like a poorly fitted transparency, laced with bitterness: *Or is Dad just such a son of a bitch that the only one he hates is me?*

His brow lifts, an unspoken question.

"He was just leaving," Dad offers, filling in the silence, and I can't even bring myself to look at him.

"Oh, cool. Well, I'm done here, so I guess I'll walk you out. I mean, I kind of have to anyway, right?"

"That other guy leave or something?"

"Ah, yeah, he was just covering for me while I was at lunch. He's normally up in . . . Well. Never mind. Come on."

Chuy moves toward the door, and I follow, nodding dimly in Dad's direction in a half-assed attempt at a farewell, trying to get my thoughts in order.

Chuy locks up behind him and starts toward the courtyard. He ambles, which I don't think I've ever really seen someone do in real life, but he moves with the slow-rolling ease of somebody who can afford to be leisurely. I can't figure him out. Everybody else I've met here—the bitchy receptionist, the inept gate security, the dour-faced guy who led me back here—I can get them. Chuy's an anomaly. He's a guy who's spending his days surrounded by the living dead and seems to like it just fine. More than that, if my dad's anything to go by; they seem to like him.

"It's cool that you came," he says when we're about halfway onto the weedy not-lawn of the courtyard. "Pretty much no one ever does. They won't tell you that at the gate, but folks just don't like to come here."

"My sister wanted to come," I say, dragging myself into the present, trying to re-orient myself in space. Trying to remember the reason I came here to begin with. "They wouldn't let her, I guess."

"Oh. That was your sister?" Chuy laughs, shaking his head.

I wince. "Yeah. Well. She's . . . opinionated."

"I mean, she's not wrong. But oh, mn. Everybody heard the shift supervisor arguing, it was the stuff of legend."

"I believe she called him an inbred bureaucrat."

"Among other things."

"I'm sure. Anyway. I was hoping . . . I mean, if that bridge isn't all well burned, that was actually what I was here for. To see if some kind of arrangement could be made, I guess. A phone call or something."

Chuy stops in place, regarding me curiously. We're just a few feet from the courtyard exit, near the path of hallways that will lead us out to the grounds and the admin single-wide. "It's important to her?"

"Yeah. I mean, he's our dad."

He studies me for a moment, and then shrugs. "Tell you what. I don't think there's a protocol in place for phone calls, but I'll look into it and I'll make it happen for you."

"Have you got that kind of power? No offense."

"They like me in here." He grins. "Not a lot of people get along well with the Undead, you know? I've got, what do you call it, rapport? A phone call shouldn't be too hard."

"I noticed nobody's outside anymore."

His smile slips. "They're working out a new system." He pulls a phone from his pocket. "You got a number?"

"What?"

"So I can let you know what they say." Chuy holds up his phone, waggles it. "I'll text you my number. You need anything, you call me direct, okay?"

I tell him my number, and soon after the vibration against my leg tells me that he's sent the message through.

"The guys at the front can be real jerks, you know? But I'll work on it for you and your sister."

"Thanks." I'm not sure what he's going to be able to accomplish, or why he's being so nice to me, but now isn't the time to look a gift horse in the mouth. So I thank him again, and head out to the admin trailer to sign myself out.

CHAPTER FIFTEEN

OUTSIDE OF THE Underground members, there are more Undead on our "pickup" list than for deliveries. Los Ojos isn't that big, and I guess it's not too surprising that it can't support more than a handful of unregistered Undead. There's me and Randy, Ash and Andrea. The Martinez brothers—Felix and Javier, though I'm still not sure which is which—and a woman named Veronica who lives on what passes for the "rich" side of town in Los Ojos terms. There's a handful of other people living nearby, names on my list that I haven't attached faces to.

Today I might actually meet some, or maybe not. Randy's text was cryptic by necessity, just an address and a time, accompanied by the message: *Coffee's on.*

Coffee, fittingly enough, is shorthand for Lazarus. I guess it makes as much sense as anything else.

The address he sent takes me to an apartment complex, fenced and gated, but the gate doesn't work; it's caught perpetually in a half-open state, like it wants to let people in but isn't fully committed to it. I roll the pickup slowly through the lot, looking at building numbers, but it's the Mercedes that tips me off first. I pull into the space beside it and try to look nonchalant as I make my way up the stairs to the second-story unit numbered 13C.

I'm not great at looking nonchalant.

I knock. After a delay, the door swings open, Randy shirtless behind it, his hair damp and sticking up in spikes. His skin is so pale it almost seems to glow; a fine fuzz of hair grows along his breastbone, darkens near his bellybutton before disappearing into the waist of his pants.

"I can take 'em off if you want," he teases, flashing a grin. "Would make us even."

"What?" I blink, gaze lifting, suddenly flustered. I remember then: Ash's bathroom, the hollow floor, the sudden grip of arms around me when I lost myself in the shower. Undead shouldn't be able to blush, but I feel something like warmth prickling over my skin, and quickly look away. There's a paper bag sitting on the kitchen bar, and I fixate on that. "That it over there?"

His apartment is smaller than I would have expected, considering his expensive car, but it's at the same level of upkeep as everything else he owns. The door opens into a living area, divided from the kitchen by a narrow counter. Piles of laundry mingle on the floor with books and empty beer cans. There's nothing on the walls, and it's sparsely furnished, just one chair in the living room sitting opposite a flat-screen TV.

"Oh, how he demurs." A wry, lopsided smile, but Randy moves toward the kitchen. "Want a beer?"

I make an inarticulate response, a throat noise sort of like an "mm-hmm," but it wouldn't matter, he'd bring me one whatever I said.

He digs a can of Pabst from the fridge and nudges the door shut with a hip, continuing on from the earlier conversation as if there'd been no interruption. "But yeah. That's the lot of it." He frowns. "There's not much, to be honest. I counted it out, an' if we hit everybody in the Underground, there's enough there to make it a week, if we stretch doses."

"Just the Underground?"

"Yeah." He sighs. "I'm talkin' with some folks, we might find some more by the end of the weekend."

I reach for the bag, feel its heft. It's not as heavy as I would've liked.

"Anyway. The receipts are inside, with the addresses. Should be easy enough. Nobody you haven't met yet." He takes a long

154

swig from his beer can, brows furrowed into a thoughtful frown. "You didn't see a black Mazda parked out front, did you?"

"I don't think so. I wasn't really paying attention. Why?"

"Martinez brothers," Randy replies, and his nose wrinkles as if disgusted. "Keep an eye out. They shouldn't know where I live, but, well."

"But well what?"

He shrugs. "Just keep an eye out. Try not to let them hassle you. They got theirs last week, they can budget their shit like everybody else." He moves away from the kitchen, setting down his beer, and fishes a shirt out from among the piles on the floor, sniffing it. He pulls it on, beginning to button it. "I'll keep working on getting a Lazarus hookup big enough to get them off our ass."

I think of Chuy, his number programmed into my phone. There's got to be more drugs available in the Lazarus House than anywhere in the state, and I know he's got access to them. But would he do it? Or would he call his coworkers, get somebody in a van to come pick me up, drag me into a room across the hall from my dad or force me into a room with him, however that works?

They know where I live. They have my address. There's no way I can risk it.

I swallow back rising bile and take the bag out to the car, prepared to deliver drugs to zombies like some weird inverted Santa Claus.

Even though I've been there before, I'm grateful for the directions to Ash's house. I doubt I could have found it otherwise, in the twists and permutations of side roads. I hadn't exactly been paying close attention the first time.

The trailer itself, though, is familiar. Lilith is outside stringing clothes on a line as I pull up, and she seems to go stiff, drawing the clothes against her chest like a protective barrier until I get out and she sees who I am. She starts to relax, looking less like a frightened rabbit, and manages to wave.

"Didn't recognize you," she says as I approach the chain-link fence. "Nice truck."

"Thanks." I offer a smile, lingering by the hood. The brown paper bag of Lazarus is stuffed below the passenger seat, and I'm not sure of the best way to hand it off. Is there a protocol to follow here, or do I just carry the bag in? This isn't exactly the kind of job that comes with training, at least not when Randy's the one in charge. "Ash home?"

She chuckles at that, and I guess, now that I think about it, that's a pretty silly question. Where else would Ash be?

"Inside," she nods toward the door. "Let yourself in, I'll be right there."

"You want some help?" I gesture toward the laundry basket, the drooping line.

She laughs again, shaking her head. "Bless your heart," she says, but nothing more, and I guess that means no.

Hesitating a moment longer, I open the passenger side, dig around for the bag and find that there are several plastic containers inside: tubs that once held margarine, or whipped cream, or guacamole. I give one a tentative shake, hearing the clink of bottles. Good enough.

I carry this inside with me, setting it down on the heavily-scratched table in the trailer's dining area. Ash is in the kitchen, standing on a chair beneath a burned-out overhead light, trying to brace himself with one hand against the ceiling as he works at the bulb. The bulb doesn't seem to want to come loose. He fidgets with it for a while, growing increasingly agitated.

He looks different, somehow. Bad. Like he's gotten older. I don't know how that's possible. The Undead don't really age, they just get . . . deader. But with Lazarus, that's not really supposed to happen either. Still, there's something drawn about his features, some tightness to his skin that I don't think was there before, like a corpse left to mummify in the desert. Skin pulls tight to his cheekbones; his eyes seem hollower, sunken somehow.

But he smiles at me, abandoning the light bulb quest and climbing back down from his chair. "Davin. Nice to see you. How's your sister?"

"Trying to dismantle the system, as always." I return the smile, lingering a bit awkwardly by the kitchen table, not sure if I should pull out a chair. I have more places to be today, but it seems rude to leave. Then again, it seems rude to infringe on their hospitality too, and I've done enough of that for a lifetime.

Heh. Lifetime.

"I presume you didn't drive out to deliver me a tub of margarine?" He nods toward the container on the table.

My smile slips into a grin. "You know, I'm not sure if that's part of a cunning disguise, or if Randy just didn't have anything else to put things in."

"A bit of both, I imagine." Ash pulls his chair away from the kitchen and toward the table, sitting down, and gestures for me to do the same. "How are you liking it? Having a . . . job, I guess is the way to put it. Being a part of the Underground."

I can feel my brow knitting, a frown without realizing it. A job, certainly; but I hadn't thought for a second that this meant anything beyond that. I definitely didn't see myself as being part of anything, much less some sort of resistance movement, some group of activists. A family can only support one revolutionary at a time, and it's not me.

I guess Ash reads something into my expression, because he's quick to add, "It's good to have family, even one you've cobbled together."

I already have family, I want to protest. I have more family than I can take care of, and it's really just the two of us. But I get what he means, and I don't want to argue, so I nod. "Yeah. Randy's been, ah, showing me the ropes."

"He likes you," Ash says, and there's something unreadable in his gray eyes. "He's not usually one for taking in strays."

I'm not sure what to do with that, but curiosity bites at me all the same. "No?"

"He never bought Ismael a new car, I'll put it that way."

"Oh." The embarrassment burns, the memory of a blush ghosting up my neck even if the capillaries there won't respond. I busy myself looking elsewhere, my eyes landing on the naked bulb in the kitchen. "You need help with that?"

Without waiting for affirmation, I'm out of my chair and into the kitchen. I can reach the light, just barely, if I stand on my toes. I stretch and brush my fingertips against the bulb, seeking a good grip before I start to turn it.

"You don't have to—" Ash starts, but stops himself.

The bulb resists being turned at first, the plastic casing at its base holding tight and trying to shift in the socket. But after a moment, I manage to get the bulb loose, unscrewing it steadily until it's in my hand, some sort of corroded residue powdering down on me after I get it out. I look around the kitchen questioningly for the replacement bulb, and set the used one back on the counter.

"Randy says we're running low on Lazarus," I say, trying to slip it in almost casually as I fish a new light bulb from the box on the counter. "He's working on it, I guess."

"I was afraid of that." Ash reaches for the margarine tub, popping it open to peer inside. "He hadn't mentioned a plan."

"I'm not sure he has one, honestly," I admit, frowning up at the bulb as I screw it in. Randy hadn't seemed exactly forthcoming with the details when he'd brought it up. "Just that he'd figure something out."

"There's always the Lazarus House."

His words startle me, and I nearly drop the bulb I'm trying to screw in.

If Ash notices, he doesn't mention it. He continues, "I always imagined I'd have to turn myself in, one day or another."

Lilith comes in then, empty laundry basket tucked up under her arm, and it saves me from having to come up with something to say. Because I know that his freedom, his ability to stay here with his wife and hang out laundry and change light bulbs and live a normal life, might just hinge on my courage to put my own life at risk.

And I don't know if that's a sacrifice I can make.

CHAPTER SIXTEEN

IT'S A BAD news week for the Undead.

That's probably how this will be remembered, if anyone's left to look back. I wonder about that sometimes. How history will remember us, if history will remember us at all. How people, a century from now, will look back on our lives and deaths and undeaths, and whether any of it will make more sense in hindsight.

That's one of the things I'm thinking while the television plays: How will all of this be remembered and reconciled and recorded?

But mostly what I'm thinking is, *how are we going to get out of this?*

The newscaster is saying, "An Undead woman was arrested today on counts of illegal possession and purchase of Lazarus, in what authorities suspect may be part of a bigger drug ring."

Shit. Shit. Shit.

"The woman, a Veronica Chavez of Los Ojos, New Mexico, was caught by an undercover agent attempting to trade large quantities of the life-extension drug for illegal methamphetamines."

"What the *fuck*." Zoe, curled up on the couch, is staring at the TV with an expression somewhere between disgust and horror.

She turns to look at me and catches my eye before I can turn back to the stove and look busy. I'm supposed to be cooking, but there's water boiling, empty and awaiting pasta, ignored now. The pan rattles against the stove. I'm just staring at the television, trying to get my brain to catch up with what's happening.

"It's suspected that Chavez, whose death was previously

unrecorded by the state, was part of an operation working closely with the Mexican cartel."

"It's not clear what these medications are being used for south of the border," a different person is saying, a microphone shoved into his face as he squints into the camera. The wind ruffles his hair. "Whether there's an epidemic of unregistered Undead, or if users are simply experimenting with recreational drug use. In any case, the illegal use and transport of Lazarus represents a serious health crisis. These drugs are necessary for maintaining quality of life among the Undead and in preventing disastrous outbreaks of violence."

The camera switches over, showing a now all-too-familiar image: an Undead with his brains leaking out over the concrete, officers circling him, guns drawn.

The voiceover continues: "Chavez is being investigated for a potential link to Ismael Gonzales, an Undead involved in a deadly police encounter earlier this summer."

"It doesn't make any *sense*," Zoe is protesting. She's grabbed a pillow and is holding it close to her chest, as if to shield herself from the television. "They're not saying everything. They can't be."

At the stove, the water's boiling over, sizzling against the burner.

Between the sounds of the television and Zoe's protests and the water splashing over onto the surface of the stove, I guess I don't hear the car pull up in the driveway. But the knocking is unmistakable, heavy raps against the door.

Like someone startled while watching a horror film, Zoe lets out a muffled scream.

There isn't enough Lazarus in my system right now for my heart to jump in my throat. It's barely beating as is, a sluggish lump of muscle taking up space in my chest, sludge moving like black tar through my veins. But the fear comes all the same, a deep nauseous feeling that prickles at my skin and sinks down through my ruined guts.

Undead-sniffing dogs.

The Underground.

A link to an illegal drug ring.

I can imagine them outside with perfect clarity: the uniforms, the nightsticks and guns, the snarling shepherds at the ends of short leads. I'm frozen in place, not knowing what to do, every movement feeling like it's happening in slow motion. Even the water, still boiling over on the stove, seems to churn slowly, all time condensed now into a small infinity.

It can't, in fact, be more than a minute.

"Davin." A voice, muffled by the door. "It's me, you asshole. Let me in."

The fear loosens its paralyzing hold by degrees, and I'm not consciously aware of moving toward the door until I'm standing behind it, hand on the knob, leaning forward to peer out through the slats of beveled glass. The light of the setting sun scatters through the incongruous angles, making it impossible to see clearly, but there's a flash of pink, an all-too-familiar shade.

I unlock the door, crack it open to peer outside, afraid somehow that this might be a trick.

"Christ, Davin. You been watchin' the news, or are you always just this paranoid?"

I gesture dumbly toward the television as I step away to let Randy inside. The news is still playing, but they've moved on from the story about Veronica Chavez. Numbly, I say, "Around here, we're always watching the news."

"Saves me some time, I guess." Randy crosses over the threshold of the house, immediately beginning to pace between the back of the couch and the kitchen table, making short loops within the gap. "We've got a problem."

"No shit we've got a problem." The fear, quickly dissipating, has been replaced with anger. I gesture toward the television. "Veronica Chavez just got arrested, and they're talking about bringing down a whole drug ring."

"Never mind that," he says, giving his head an irritable shake. "We have bigger problems."

I look at Randy, really, for the first time since he got here. There's something off about him; something paler than usual, maybe. His hair, usually artfully tousled in a way that looks careless, now actually is careless—it sticks out at odd angles, clusters of spikes plastered flat to his head. He missed a button on his shirt, and the collar is crooked, the top button not aligning with the hole.

I squint. It's hard to imagine something worse.

"We're out."

His words fall with greater importance than I initially give them. I don't understand what he's saying, why his tone's like that. We're out of what? I'm still caught up on the Veronica Chavez thing. I'm still thinking about police dogs at my door.

"Unless you've got a stockpile you're not telling me about," Randy says—and maybe he's taking my stunned silence for nonchalance, because he's starting to sound angry—"we're about to see real quick-like what really happens when Undead hit the limits of withdrawal."

"What?" It's Zoe who asks the question, turning to peek over the top of the couch, glasses visible over the back of it like Kilroy. "What do you mean?"

"I *mean*," Randy snaps, irritation evident in his voice, "we are shit outta luck on sellers. They're out of the game."

My brain's running sluggishly, slowing down with the early effects of withdrawal—that feverish, out-of-body feeling that comes on before the sickness—and the mental whiplash of fear, anger, shock, disbelief is overwhelming. Figuring out what to feel, how to react, is like climbing my way up out of a sinkhole. "How? What happened to everybody?"

Randy holds up a hand, folding down fingers as he recites off names I don't recognize. The details of it are mostly lost on me, names I don't know, people I didn't meet or was never introduced to. But the gist of it sinks in well enough: Skipped town. Arrested. Dodging his calls. Taken into the Lazarus

House. The stories are different, but the endpoint for us is all the same.

"Our options," he says when he's finished, ticking them off on each finger. "We can try to find a new dealer. We can go to the source ourselves. We can turn ourselves in for treatment. Or we can do nothing and maybe tear through the city."

"There's no way that's right!" Zoe protests, and she's up from her spot on the couch and heading down the hall, presumably running to her computer for answers. "There's got to be *something*."

"I'm not saying I wouldn't like a zombie apocalypse." Randy resumes pacing, circling a tight path over the carpet like a caged tiger. "Just maybe not right now."

My head's whirling. I don't like the options, but I can't see anywhere that he's wrong. There are risks on all sides. The only question left is which risk am I more willing to take: being discovered . . . or losing myself entirely?

"I . . . have an idea," I say, finally, cutting Randy off in his ranting. "I don't know if it'll work. But . . . I can try."

I didn't save Chuy's number in my phone, but his text message is still there, looking up at me cheerfully from my brief message log. It's sandwiched between Randy's unnecessarily cautious coded messages and my own frequent messages to check in with Zoe to see that she's eaten or to remind her to lock the door while I'm out.

:)

That's it. The sum total of the text, and my only connection with our last hope, is summed up in a smiley face. My thumb trembles as it hovers over the message, tapping the icon to call him.

The phone rings for a long time, and I think maybe he's not going to answer. And a part of me is relieved, because even though I need this to work, a part of me is so terrified by it that I want the choice taken away from me. If everything goes to shit somehow, despite my efforts—if I do my best and it all goes sideways anyway—I think I can live with that.

Knowing that I made it worse somehow, that I've ended up where I am as a result of my own choices . . . that's a harder thing to swallow. Shouldering the blame is a thousand times more unbearable.

I'm about to hang up when the phone makes a noise. A moment of static, background noise, and then a voice, undoubtedly Chuy's, but different somehow on the phone. Distant. Flattened. Lacking some of the warmth that comes from his eyes, or maybe that's just my imagination.

"Hello?"

"Hey, um. Chuy. It's Davin. Montoya." I stumble over the words, feeling like an idiot. I should have planned what I was going to say. I should have thought about this. Through the wall of my bedroom, I can hear the clack of keys in Zoe's room, the frenetic typing as she looks for a different solution.

"Yeah, hey, Davin. I remember. You kept my number." There's a shift in his voice, familiarity, something that sounds like a smile. "What's up?"

"Well, um. You said to let you know if I needed anything." I hesitate. I don't know how to ask this. "Can we meet up some place? I think I need to see you."

"Yeah?"

The way the question hangs at the end of the word makes me grimace. It lilts upward like a flirtation.

Shit. I try to think of a way to make it sound less like I'm asking him out. "Maybe we can grab a cup of coffee?" That's not helping. "There's a place called CJ's downtown, if you've heard of it . . . ?"

A moment of silence that seems to stretch out for a very long time. Then, "Yeah, I know where it is." There's a roughness to this admission, a heaviness. He's silent, but I don't rush to fill the silence. When he speaks again, it's weary, lacking the warmth and flirtation that had peeked in a moment prior. "How much do you need?"

"Excuse me?"

"Lazarus," Chuy says. "That's what this is about, right?"

My heart, already sluggish, stutters to a halt. It merely hangs there, a dead weight in my chest, swollen against my ribs. I forget how to breathe. The air catches in my throat, an uncomfortable bubble that refuses to move either in or out, caught in stasis. Time, like my body, stands still.

Against my silence, Chuy continues: "You're good. You pass well. I wasn't sure until right now. I kind of had an idea, but I thought, no way, Chuy, you're crazy. But CJ's, man? Everybody who works with Undead knows what that place is. You trying to get killed?"

My throat works, trying to dislodge the stale air that's settled in my mouth, my throat, suffocating. My eyes burn, but I'm afraid to blink. I'm afraid if I close them, they might never open again. Like seeing the room around me is the only thing left tethering me to reality; like I might fall into the darkness forever if I let myself get a glimpse of it.

I focus on my lungs, imagine them in my chest like two over-filled balloons, swollen and blocked. I force myself to exhale, the air escaping in a long, fetid sigh. An agonal gasp, they call it; the last long breath a corpse takes, long after the brain has died and the body has started to shut down. Dogs do it, when the euthanasia fluid circulates through their veins. The vet warns you not to be alarmed. They're not in pain, they tell you. They're already gone by the time it happens.

But not me.

"You still there?"

I make a sound. I hope it sounds affirmative.

"So you got the money, yeah?"

"We . . . have money," I rasp, with effort. The last of the air in my lungs whispers out, leaving the whisper of a wheeze, a sibilant hiss that hangs awkwardly at the end of the sentence.

"Are you . . . going . . . ?" I swallow. Lick my lips. Try to bring myself back to the present. Cigarette burns ripple at the edges of my vision, little spots of darkness, and I'm afraid I might black out. But I heave in another breath, and I feel dead, but a little less dead than before. The fear slowly starts to loosen its grip.

"I'm not going to tell anyone," Chuy says, almost impatient. "But you gotta be careful, *esé*. You get caught out, and it's not just your ass on the line, you know?"

My body's only barely coming back into my control. My brain feels fuzzy at the edges. "You . . . you're not fucking with me? You'll do it?"

"Yeah, man. I'm surprised, honestly. You just die recently or something?" He laughs. I'm not sure what's funny. "Two days. Let me tell you where to meet."

He tells me a place, a certain park in a neighboring town, a reservation border town near the casino. He tries to give me directions twice, then gives up, tells me to look it up. Asks if I have GPS. Everything is surreal in its normalcy. We set a time. He quotes me a price. The details are starting to blur sideways. I remember, too late, to try to write it down, grabbing for the laptop tucked under my bed. I think I get it all down. I hope so.

I hang up, feeling the sort of visceral emptiness that can only come from a deep and terrible relief. It's the way I felt when the hospital called to tell me that Mom had died. The emptiness of grief, filling up with the knowledge that, at last, the struggle was over; that I didn't have to worry anymore.

My problems are solved, maybe. Or they're not, and it's all about to go to hell. Maybe it's a setup. Maybe he's going to meet us with cops, Lazarus House guards, snarling dogs or guns pressed up into our faces. Maybe it's all over for us all.

But it's out of my hands now, and I fall back into my pillow and let the empty euphoria of relief wash over me.

It's an awful, guilty feeling, and it settles in my guts as I set the phone aside and stare at the darkness overhead. Lazarus cravings gnaw at me, restless and feverish. My skin crawls with them.

Deep inside, some primal part of me squirms and threatens to awaken.

Over the next two days, a plan begins to take form. We develop it in bits and snatches. Randy's in and out of the house, talking to us, talking to the Underground, coordinating. Zoe spends every second of free time at the computer, researching something with greater focus and enthusiasm than usual—an almost frantic energy, an obsessiveness I recognize as emotional avoidance.

We don't talk about what might happen if I can't get hold of more Lazarus. If this whole thing goes sideways, or if Chuy can't really be trusted. I keep trying to bring it up, but she always manages to deflect.

We're cutting it awfully close. It's been two days since my last Lazarus dose—since *any* of us have had any. I'm not feeling the withdrawal as harshly yet, not the real bad bits, but I'm afraid it'll set in before we get the chance to meet Chuy.

Randy insists that the withdrawal doesn't always set in on the third day. If you've been on it a while, he says, or if you were taking enough that the residue lingers in your system, it could take days. A week or two, maybe. We might have plenty of time.

I hope he's right.

"Maybe it's not even a big deal," Zoe's saying, the night before the drop has been scheduled. She's in the living room with us, curled on the couch with a pillow held to her chest. It's the most I've seen of her all week. She looks good—hopeful—satisfied, perhaps, with whatever answers she's found for herself. "I mean, maybe the media's full of bullshit. You said as much when we first met, right?" Her eyes land on Randy, eager, searching for validation or comfort.

Randy's pacing the kitchen, pawing through the contents of the cabinets. Occasionally he pulls something down to inspect it, sniffing containers and nibbling the corners of crackers. His nose wrinkles in distaste. He makes a noncommittal noise. "I said it *could* be bullshit. To be honest, I don't know for sure what could happen. I do know that withdrawal is terrible. More terrible than anything. It's worse than death. And I'd know."

"I've heard there are Undead who are fine," Zoe adds, unperturbed. "Who've been off Lazarus and have zero issues."

"Where did you hear that?" Randy opens a jar of peanut butter, sniffs, grimaces.

Zoe looks suddenly embarrassed, color rising in her cheeks. " . . . The Dusty Bones."

Randy snorts.

"Wait. Who are the Dusty Bones?" I ask, feeling out of my depth.

"Just some old weirdos on the forum," Randy says dismissively. "Nobody knows who they are. They show up sometimes, rant about some crazy shit, disappear. They could be anybody. For all I know, they're not even Undead." His gaze rolls over to Zoe, glinting with an edge of sharp humor. "It might come as a surprise, kid, but it turns out not everybody is who they say they are online."

"I know that. I'm just . . . " She shrugs vaguely, desperately. This conversation isn't going the way she'd hoped it would. "You were real. I'm real. Here we are."

"Out of curiosity," I ask, feeling something like hope start to stir up and wanting to squash it as soon as possible, "do you actually know anybody who's gone . . . you know. Like the guys on the news."

"Not, like, close personal friends or anything. But I've heard stories. All the usual urban legend shit, but some things I tend to believe. We used to have this one guy, he was our drug runner before Izzy. It's been so long I can't even remember his damn name. But I do remember he was this scrawny, quiet nerd type. Great for sending out to meet with dealers. This was before we got most of our shit by skimming. When we didn't have the connections to get it at the source."

It hasn't escaped my attention that people in my line of work don't seem to last very long.

Randy moves away from the kitchen, leaning over the back

of the couch so he's between me and Zoe. "Now, I wasn't there for this, so I didn't see this in person. But the story goes that he lost his shit on the dealer. Not your usual disagreement over money stuff. Completely crazy. Tore his throat out with his teeth."

"Jesus."

"That's the story, anyway. I don't know where he ended up after that, to be honest. I do know that we needed a new dealer after that. *Something* killed him. I think the story checks out."

"But if he was buying Lazarus," Zoe says, wide-eyed behind her glasses, "why would he even be going through withdrawals in the first place?"

"Honestly? Money, probably. My guess is he figured he could get by without it, and there was a whole lot of money to be had in pocketing some off each deal and selling for himself. There's a whole black market economy out there, you know."

I shudder, imagining teeth stained with blood, long fingers digging into flesh.

Sudden rage syndrome, I think, remembering that damn dog, the spaniel with something broken in her head. *It's just a thing that happens sometimes.*

Sometimes they have to be put down.

CHAPTER SEVENTEEN

"**C**AN I COME?"

"What? Zoe, *no*. Why would you even ask that?"

It's Friday night, and we're running late. It's going to be a long drive, and I don't know my way around the town out there; I'm expecting us to get lost, and that'll make us even later. I don't know how long Chuy will wait up, and I'm terrified of texting him in case he decides to give up on us.

Randy's late. He's not replying to my messages. A thousand explanations run through my head, and I like each one a little less than the one before. I'm starting to think maybe I should go to his apartment. Maybe I should drive out to meet Chuy by myself. Maybe something terrible has happened.

"You'll be fine," Zoe says, but beneath her outward confidence I can hear a hint of fear. She's trying to convince herself as much as me.

"Yeah."

I want to sound confident, to comfort her, but it's hard to do it when all I can think about is all of the ways this could go wrong. I can't stop imagining my face pasted over Izzy's body, leaking blood and brains onto the concrete. I can't stop thinking of the woman snarling into the camera, of a body bent double over roadkill in the shine of headlights.

An image, so intense it's like a craving: Me, sinking my teeth into Zoe, tearing at her flesh, losing myself entirely like some television monster.

I don't want to do this, but I *have* to do this.

I'm lighting up yet another cigarette when Randy finally rolls up. Headlights wash over me and Zoe on the front porch. I get up, start toward the car before Randy's even gotten it into park.

"Go inside," I tell her. "Lock the door. We'll be back as soon as we can."

"Good luck," she says, and then, impulsively, as if moving on an afterthought, she jumps up to wrap her arms around my shoulders in a fierce hug. I freeze, startled, but return the hug. I hope she doesn't notice that I'm shaking.

"I'll see you tonight," I say, mustering a smile, and then dive for Randy's car.

He mutters a greeting, not quite words.

"The fuck have you been?" I ask.

"Sorry. I'll explain on the way." He looks disheveled, his pink hair tousled and standing up oddly. He seems even paler than usual, the bruise at his throat thick and black in the darkness of the car. "I sure hope we've got this in the bag tonight," he says, shifting into reverse. "Because we've got a long fuckin' night ahead of us otherwise."

"Withdrawal setting in on you, too?"

The first time withdrawals hit, they came on so quickly and so unexpectedly that I didn't notice or realize what was really happening. I'd just felt sick, feverish, like the worst case of the flu. But this time I'm hyper-aware of every detail, and it's terrible.

Here's the thing nobody tells you about being dead: it hurts, worse than anyone could ever describe. Your body's in a constant struggle against the unnatural forces keeping it in motion. The reanimation virus doesn't care about your feelings; it just gets you up and moving, with no regard for the consequences. Your heart and lungs keep doing their magic, pumping blood and oxygen to your muscles and feeding your brain, but you're rotting away from the inside, and you can feel it. It aches like the dry socket of a rotten tooth, but everywhere.

"Do you think it always feels like this?" I ask a few miles out, without preamble. "I mean, when you go off it. The people who go crazy. Do you think they feel this way all the time?"

"Maybe." Randy's eyes are firm on the road. "Maybe that's

why they start killing people. If I had to feel like this forever, I'd probably kill people too."

Another thing no one warns you about: Once the drug wears off, the trembling starts, and the fear sets in. At this point, I can't tell where natural anxiety ends and the withdrawal-induced paranoia begins. The fear is eternity, a snake eating its tail.

I keep forgetting to breathe. My heart only beats intermittently, like it's mostly forgotten how. You can make your lungs work, if you force them. If you concentrate, you can fill and empty them, the balloon-like sacs that occupy space and cling tight to your ribs. But you can't do anything with your heart. You can't will it into beating.

My hands are cold, blue-gray under the skin. I feel deader than I did that day out on the bridge, the first time I folded myself into Randy's passenger seat, bleeding and dripping puked-up viscera onto the upholstery. Deader, of course, because I've been dead this whole time. Decaying, subtly, in ways that aren't expressed in the death of cells and tissue.

Randy keeps looking into the rearview mirror.

"So what's up?" I ask, and it takes an effort to say it, words needing to be formed with precision, breath controlled—all those things that are second nature when you're alive. Conscious decisions now, every agonizing one of them, and it's a challenge to remember to prioritize breathing and forming words.

"Martinez brothers," he replies. His accent is thicker than usual, and there's something almost sleep-logged about his voice. I realize, after a moment, that it's like he's being strangled; like the rope that left the bruises around his throat is back, tightening. "Thought I saw 'em earlier, when I was leaving my place. Took the long way to your house, thinkin' I'd try to lose 'em."

"Are you sure?"

He shakes his head. Then, almost as punctuation to his uncertainty, he paws around in the center console for his cigarettes and shakes out a couple, lighting them both before handing me one. His hands are shaking. I don't know if it's fear or withdrawal, or maybe both. But I take the cigarette and start to keep an eye on the mirrors too, watching uneasily for the glow of headlights.

There's a tense few minutes as a pair of headlights loom in the mirror, spots of light that make it impossible to make out the car behind us or its driver. Randy slows, as if hoping the car will pass, but it lingers there behind us, riding our ass.

The casino looms up on the right side, a garish display of light and color against the darkness of the desert backdrop. The car behind us peels off at the exit, its headlights finally averted as it pulls away and navigates down into the parking lot.

We let out a collective sigh of relief, but it's short-lived. The anxiety starts to creep back in; insidious, pervasive. Randy drives in silence, and I squirm in the passenger seat, watching the world slowly roll past.

As if summoned, the Rio de Animas looms ahead, the bridge suddenly the only part of this landscape that seems starkly familiar. I can see the missing guard rail, the place where my car flew over the edge and down into the ravine below. My car might still be down there somewhere, the exoskeleton of an alien insect, defeated and abandoned on some cosmic battlefield.

My eyes move side to side, quickly scanning the area for signs of life. But, of course, there are no hunched-over figures crouched in the road, no shadowy men looming over the bodies of carrion.

There probably never had been.

"Hey, Randy. Have you ever heard about skinwalkers out here?"

"Davin, I'm from Georgia."

"Well, right, but . . . " I trail off. "Never mind. It's stupid. It's just, the night I died." I falter, fall silent again. I can't think of how to explain, or why I'm even bothering to, when there are so many bigger things to worry about right now. At least the talking is coming a little easier, now that I'm starting to get the hang of it. It takes a lot of focus, coordinating breathing and speaking, but every word isn't the bitter struggle it had been earlier. I don't know how long that'll last.

Randy doesn't push. Instead he waits, allowing the silence to stretch, waiting perhaps to see if I'll take the time to fill it. Then: "Nobody asks how you died." Words that echo something he told me when we first met. "But it always comes out, eventually."

I can see it so clearly in my head, the figure bent double in the rain. The feeling of tires losing their grip on wet asphalt, the spinning, the pain of impact. But instead, I say, "So. Skinwalkers. They're, like, shapeshifters. They're people who can turn into animals."

"So, werewolves?"

"No, not . . . not like werewolves." I frown, trying to think. "There's a lot of different stories. They're supposed to be witches, in Navajo culture. They can steal your body by looking you in the eye."

In my grandmother's version, these witches were people born with an animal soul; there was something wrong with them, something beastly, and it drove them from the tribe and into solitude. And there they lived, crouching in the rocks of the mesa, naked and draped in furs. In her stories, they crawled on all fours and ate raw meat, and in the night you could sit outside and hear their terrible howls and screams rising up into the night.

I've heard other myths about skinwalkers, in passing; myths more accurate to their native folklore, the culture that birthed them. But those aren't the stories of my childhood. They weren't the stories of a frightened seven-year-old, pressed against the passenger side door of an old pickup, peering with wide eyes at the road just outside the gleam of headlights to catch a glimpse of a naked, fur-draped man or a dog standing on two legs.

Even Dad believed in skinwalkers. He didn't think they were witches or shapeshifters, but he did believe that there were people—wild people—who lived out on the edges of the town. The way he told it, sometimes babies were born "wrong"—deformed—and they were given over to the wild people of the desert. Whenever we drove through Mesa Road, Dad would

175

always lock the doors, like a reflex; I don't even think he knew he was doing it.

It sounds absurd to say any of this out loud. Even a pair of zombies driving a sports car to a drug deal has some limits, and Randy comes from such a different world that I don't know how to bridge it. I don't know how to explain to him that there's the myth, and then there's the story that gets passed around like common knowledge, and that the thing that has me afraid right now is only partly about witches and partly about death.

"Okay. So skinwalkers," Randy prompts, and he sounds interested, or maybe just eager for a change in subject, a distraction from the stress of our mission.

"Yeah. It's just . . . I saw something, or thought I saw something, the night I died. I don't know. It's stupid. Forget about it."

He starts to say something, but then leans forward, squinting at an exit sign. "Hey. Is this us?"

A moment later, we pull off, retreating from the highway and down onto an old country road, a pockmarked stretch of asphalt that doesn't look like it's had maintenance in a decade.

Passing rows of houses—some shabby single-wides like Ash's, some old adobe, some modified aluminum shacks—I realize how ridiculous we must look in this damn car. I hope nobody's awake to look out their windows right now, because it'd be pretty easy to get suspicious about a pink-haired white boy rolling through the rez in a sports car this time of night.

"What's the deal with this car, anyway?" I ask as Randy fiddles with his phone, checking the address.

"Part of my hush money deal," he explains. "Dad figures if he can cover my rent, keep me in a nice car, give me some spending money, I'll be motivated to stay hidden out here. Figures that's enough to keep me from ruining his reputation back home." He grins. It's only a little hollow. "I get a little bit more in election years. That's pretty nice."

Up ahead, a shopping center: a drug store, a liquor store, a tire store. Beyond that, a copse of trees clustered unnaturally for New Mexico. Implants. A park.

We're not alone, though. As Randy pulls close, we see two other cars, parked next to each other, facing opposite directions so their drivers' windows align. They're in the center of the parking lot, and Randy hesitates as we approach, the car slowing practically to a stop.

"You've got to be fucking kidding me," he whispers.

"What?"

Randy nods at the cars in the lot: one a gray Corolla, the other a black Mazda. It's too dark to see clearly inside, but against the glow of a single overhead street lamp, I can make out two shapes in one car, one in the other.

"That's the Martinez brothers. I've seen that car parked outside my house enough times to know."

"There's no way. They couldn't have followed us here. We would have seen."

"Unless he's dealin' with 'em, too." He snorts, an angry, derisive sound. "How many people do you think he invited out here?"

Randy steps down on the gas, speeding up to pass the park. The road ahead ends in a cul-de-sac, and Randy mutters a curse under his breath as we're forced to turn around and drive back the other way, as if we weren't conspicuous enough already.

"Wait. Let's just stop here," I say, nodding to the shadowy side of the street. "Let's just watch for a second."

He cuts the headlights, and we creep forward in the dark, across the street from the parking lot where the two cars are still parked side by side. A door opens, a tall shape unfolding from the Corolla—I can't see his face, but the silhouette is familiar enough, a brawny expanse that I figure has got to be Chuy. He circles around to the back of the car, facing us now, and leans back against the trunk of the car. His eyes are shaded by distance and the shadows cast by the street lamp, but I imagine he must be looking at us.

The shadows in the other car are, for the moment, still.

"Do you think it's a trap?" I ask, twisting anxiously in the passenger seat. I hadn't anticipated anyone else being here. I'd kind of assumed that the purpose of meeting in the park at night was privacy.

"Only one way to find out, I guess," Randy mutters, and heaves the driver's side door open, circling the car to cross the street. I follow after, lifting a hand to wave.

"You're late," Chuy says, and then looks at Randy, frowning. "Who's this?"

"My ride," I say, and glance sideways at the Mazda as we approach. "Who are they?"

"Just some other Undead. Same as you."

The Mazda's doors swing open then, and sure enough, the brothers from that day at CJ's. They're dressed differently—no more flannel or bandanas—but I recognize them well enough. One's wearing a white wifebeater and jeans. The other one, with the full-sleeve tattoo, is wearing a jean jacket over a faded t-shirt. Felix and Javier, but I never can remember who's who.

"Hope you ain't been waiting on our account," Randy says, glancing between Chuy and the brothers. He's easily the smallest person here and sticks out more than a little, between his pale skin and pink hair and the Oxford shirt, sleeves rolled at the cuffs.

"No way. We just got here." The guy with the tattoos—I think that's Javier—nudges him, hand on his shoulder. "What I'm wondering, though, is if you were gonna let us know this was happening."

"Kind of seems like you were gonna cut us out," Felix, maybe, says. He shifts his weight, and the hem of his wifebeater lifts, showing a snub-nosed pistol tucked into the waistband of his pants. I don't think that's an accident.

"Cut you out of what?" Randy snorts. "There's nothing to cut you out of yet."

I lay a hand on Randy's back, trying to quiet him, and turn plaintively toward Chuy. "Look. I don't care who's buying, as long as you've got the stuff. Please."

"Eyy, we're not trying to start shit," Javier says. He runs a hand through his greased-back hair. "Just being sure we all get what we're owed, yeah?"

Chuy looks at me, and there's some emotion in his eyes that's visible even in the dark, even with the stark shadows cast by the street lamp. It looks like disappointment, maybe, but it flickers and is gone, disappearing as he turns to pop open the trunk. "Yeah, yeah, relax. I've got it. At great risk to my livelihood, I'll have you know."

"Yeah, well, it'll be a great risk to a whole lot of lives real soon if one of us starts tearing through the city," Randy mutters.

Javier makes a sound, low in his throat. Agreement, probably, but it sounds more like a growl than anything.

Chuy seems to hesitate for a moment, but reaches into the trunk and pulls out a container. He pops open the lid, and glass vials inside capture the light, glistening beneath the street lamp.

The craving wells up in me, desperate and longing, a physical sensation that starts somewhere deep in my ruined guts and runs up my spine. My mouth almost begins to water with the proximity of the Lazarus and the promise of how I might feel as soon as it's in my body.

It's so close. We're so close. Just some money that needs to exchange hands, and then this nightmare will be over.

Except.

"How do we know it's legit?" Javier asks. "For all I know, it's water in there or something. I'm not paying for water."

"For fuck's sake," Randy mutters.

"I thought you'd say that." Chuy sighs and digs around in his trunk again, emerging with a capped syringe. He tosses this to Javier, who catches it in one hand and twirls it like a pencil between his fingers. "Please. Feel free to sample it."

Headlights wash over us.

Another car rolls by, coming down the path in the same route that we came down. It slows as it passes the park, and I can make out the silhouette of someone leaning out of the driver's side. I can feel eyes on us. But they keep driving, pulling off onto a side road.

Just another drug deal in the park, they're probably thinking. Business as usual. All the same, I hope they hurry this up.

Randy's thinking the same thing. "As entertaining as this is, and believe me, I'm captivated," he mutters, a hand thrust into his pocket, balled into a fist around the cash inside, "can we just pay for our shit and go?"

Felix fingers the gun at his waist, pulls it out with a sort of well-practiced, measured nonchalance. "There some reason you don't want to wait?"

"You mean, aside from that we're all standing out here like a big fuckin' sign saying, 'Yo, illegal activity happening here'?" Randy's more willing to mouth off to a guy with a gun than I am, but then, I guess being dead for a while helps eliminate some give-a-damn.

While they bicker, Javier's loading the syringe, prodding for the vein in his forearm. He slides the needle under the skin, depresses the plunger. His eyes flutter closed, jaw hanging slack with the telltale signs of immediate relief. His complexion, naturally tanned, grows flush; it's like someone turning up the saturation on an image. A smile tugs at the edge of his lips.

And that's when everything goes to hell.

Javier's eyes snap open, but there's something there that wasn't before, or maybe something that's gone missing. Like a switch flipped somewhere, a shift toggled between "human" and "inhuman." Though his cheeks are flushed with life, his eyes are like a corpse's, flat and empty.

But I don't have long to stare at his eyes, because within seconds of opening them, he's lunged forward. I grab Randy by the collar, jerking him backwards and out of the way, and Javier collides with Chuy.

Chuy lets out a surprised sound, not quite a scream, and stumbles backward. Javier's on him like a dog, his hands grasping at his throat, his teeth bared back as he grabs fistfuls of

Chuy's shirt. I see them go down, Chuy slamming back into the still-open trunk of his Corolla. His head snaps back against the open trunk lid, a smear of blood staining the metal lip, but that's all I can see before Javier's on him, climbing up his body like he's scaling a fence.

All of this takes a matter of seconds.

"Javi? Javi? Oh shit, man! *Ay dios mio!*" Felix, gun in hand, reels backward. His eyes bulge. For a moment, he seems to forget where he is, what's happening. He clutches his hands to his head, gun still in one fist, an expression of dumbfounded horror inscribed over his face.

I grasp for Randy with my other hand, tugging him backwards because he seems rooted to the spot. We stumble back together, and I almost lose my footing. I'm feeling woozy, uncertain on my feet; the ground seems to sway under me.

But from the trunk, echoing up from within the metal frame, Chuy is screaming. And there are other sounds: wet, unpleasant sounds. Things I don't want to think about.

Then, like fireworks being shot off—*pop pop pop!* Gunfire. Felix has remembered his gun, but he's firing wildly. I don't know if he's trying to miss on purpose, or if he's so panicked that he can't choose between shooting and scrambling backwards. He makes a dive for his car, shooting back over his shoulder, and that, at least, is enough to rouse Randy from his sluggish response.

We turn and run for the Mercedes parked across the street. We make it, Randy struggling with his keys, punching the button to unlock the door just as I see Javier—or what had been Javier—swinging his head around, lips curling up. The street lamp glints off his teeth.

I dive into the passenger seat, bang my knees painfully on the dash as I cram myself in. "Go, go, go!" I urge.

Randy struggles to get his key in the ignition. Across the street, Javier has abandoned Chuy, or whatever's left of Chuy; all I can see is a dark shape sprawled halfway inside the trunk. He's started to run for us. Felix is still standing outside his car, mouth

181

open in a slack "O" of horror, and I realize Javier must have the keys.

Not our problem.

Javier makes a run for us, and Felix extends his arm, snub-nosed pistol aimed in our direction or Javi's, it's hard to know for sure.

Randy floors the gas, and the tires squeal. Javier hits the asphalt of the street, picks up speed as he approaches. I try to flatten myself against the seat, hand scrambling for the recliner lever.

Pop! Pop! Pop!

The thud of bullets against metal, like heavy hail. The crunch of glass, inches away from my face. A blast of air as the window shatters, the air pressure in the car suddenly shifting.

The car gathers momentum and lurches forward, and the outside world is a sudden blur.

"Shit. Randy! Are you okay?"

"I'm fine." His voice sounds thick, rasping like he's speaking through a sore throat, and I struggle to get a closer look at him but it's so dark in the cabin I can barely see his face.

We drive, jumping onto the first side street we can. I hope he knows where he's going; I hope we don't turn a circle out here in the labyrinthine trails of unfamiliar county roads. When we make it back onto the highway, it's like letting out a breath I'd been holding the entire time; my body seems to deflate, and all that's left inside is trembling, the afterburn of terror.

CHAPTER EIGHTEEN

WE END UP at the casino.

I don't think it was a conscious decision. Randy had peeled out onto the highway and just kept driving until the bright lights filled the night sky. It's not a bad plan, though: it's air-conditioned, well-lit, and crowded. It's also open all night, so we have a place to hide out for a while. It's better than trying to go home, better than trying to hold it together long enough to last a long drive through darkness and desert.

"Were we followed?" he asks as he cuts the engine and heaves himself outside, barely keeping to his feet as he hits the ground.

I turn to look through the empty window, the image framed by the ragged edges of shattered glass. The road seems deserted: no approaching headlights, no low-profile dark cars creeping up through the night. No shambling corpses, animalistic figures waiting to spring out from the night. I don't know who's left to follow us. Javier didn't look like he'd be in a position to drive ever again. Chuy's almost certainly dead. With us gone as a distraction, I imagine Felix isn't in any better shape. "I don't think so."

A few shards of safety glass come loose as I open the door, wobbling like teeth that fall out when I close it behind me.

"Good. Let's get inside."

I hesitate, eyeballing the gaping wound of the busted window. Twin bullet holes in the passenger side door, the bullets still embedded inside the metal.

"If somebody wants to steal the fuckin' car, they can help themselves," Randy rasps. "I'll make insurance handle it."

He clears his throat, bracing himself against the open driver's door as he starts to cough, hacking up something that's come loose from down inside his throat. He spits up a dark glob, some combination of old blood and mucus and tissue, and it splatters against the asphalt. He wipes the back of his hand across his mouth and it comes away smeared with blood.

We hurry inside.

It's late, so the crowd is thin, but there are still plenty of people here—the usual crowd of lonely, desperate people who fill seats at slot machines in the early morning hours. The hobbyists and celebrators have gone home; the drunks have wandered away to sleep it off in a corner somewhere, or else find their next fix. What's left are the elderly; the disabled; the lonely people whose lives have fallen apart; and the desperate people who come here to give their hopes a place to die.

No one looks at us as we pass, and we're surrounded by the incessant jumble of sound, the flash of color, things buzzing and ringing and, beneath that, the steady thrum of canned music piped in to cover the passage of time.

Without talking, we make our way to the bathroom. Randy collapses against the wall, slowly sliding down until he's seated on the tile. I lean against the sink and let out a deep sigh, air escaping my lungs. It smells like dry rot, like something's dead inside me. Which, of course, it is.

Neither of us says anything for a long time. I'm still shaking. Randy's quiet, still; I don't see him trembling, but for the first time since I've met him, he's not smirking either.

"What the actual fuck was that?" he asks, finally.

"I don't know," I admit.

"He went fucking crazy. He was *biting* him."

"It doesn't make any sense." I don't want to remember what I just saw, but it plays back incessantly in my mind anyway. "It . . . it couldn't be withdrawal. Javier turned *after* he injected it. I saw him. He looked fine . . . for a minute."

"Maybe there was something wrong with the Lazarus," Randy says, but doesn't sound convinced.

Silence settles between us for a while. We sit opposite each other on the bathroom floor, the sounds of the casino a distant echo beyond the door, and share in the silence and the horror for what feels like a very long time.

Eventually, I notice something weird about the way his shirt's hanging on his body. It's wet, damp; a dark stain spreads in a circle near his armpit.

"You're hurt," I say.

"I didn't notice," Randy says, with an edge of wonder in his voice. "I can't feel it."

I know what he means. I can't feel much of anything right now either.

"Take off your shirt."

"What?" He tries for humor, weakly. "You're not even goin' to take me out to dinner first?"

It falls flat. I look at him, waiting, tired.

He lifts up his shirt, pulling it over his head. There's a wound in his side, oozing dark fluids, and I lean in close to take a look. There's a weird feeling, an inverted déjà vu; I guess it's about time I'm the one leaning in to try and rescue him instead of the other way around. Not that there's a lot I can do just now, not when the two of us are huddled in a men's room at a tribal casino in the small hours of the morning.

"I don't think the bullet's in there," I say, squinting at the wound. "It looks like it just grazed you."

"It's probably in the seat somewhere," he says.

I grab a handful of paper towels and run them under warm water. Dab at the jagged edges of his flesh, gently probe at the insides. He doesn't wince or cry out, just stares straight ahead, a thoughtful look clouding his dark eyes.

I toss the damp towels, now stained red-black, into the trash. I pull out some fresh towels and press them up against the wound, staunching the oozing blood. What I really need is a needle and thread, something to stitch it up with.

"Don't suppose you've got a suture kit in your pocket?"

"No." A pause, a beat, an attempt at a feeble smile. "I'm just happy to see you."

Our eyes meet then, for the first time since all of this started, and I can't stop the laughter from coming. It bubbles up out of my throat and pours out, hysterical. I'm laughing so hard tears are leaking from the corners of my eyes, and my whole body's shaking. I fall back against the wall next to him, leaving him to hold the paper towels in place against his side, and laugh until my voice starts to go out.

Randy's laugh is a dry wheeze, a bark that shakes his body. He snorts, and tries to stifle it with a hand, which only makes him laugh harder. Between hysterical peals, he gasps out a whisper, thick with the accent he usually tries so hard to hide. "Aw, honey. We are *so* fucked."

CHAPTER NINETEEN

WHEN THE LAUGHTER fades, all that's left inside is a hollow ache, an emptiness that digs down deep inside. We eventually leave the bathroom, Randy with his bloody shirt pulled back on, me with shards of safety glass in my shoes, my hair. An old lady looks at us strangely as we pass, making our way to the front doors; she's smoking, and through the blue haze her eyes are sharp and judgmental.

But we leave unmolested, and find the car just as we left it. The parking lot is all but deserted, like the highway. Even the truckers have pulled off to go to sleep by now.

At highway speeds, the broken window is more than a nuisance. The wind whips at my face, ruffles my hair, steals my voice. I'm a little glad, at least, for the excuse not to carry on conversation. I don't know what I could say. My mind's just going over and over what happened, trying to make sense of it. The fear about that makes a figure eight, circling and twining with my anxiety about what's going to happen next.

When we get home, the house is dark and quiet. It won't be long until dawn, and Zoe is asleep on the couch at an odd angle, like she was trying to stay up and slumped over, succumbing to exhaustion. She's still wearing her glasses, and they're askew, one earpiece loose and tangling in her hair.

I go to fetch a blanket from the hall closet, drape it over her. Take off her glasses, fold them, set them on the coffee table. No point in disturbing her; she'll have questions, and I don't want to answer them. I don't know if I can right now. I don't know how to begin explaining to her all of the things that happened, or what they might mean for us now. It's not something that I understand.

I nod for Randy to follow me down the hall into the bathroom, and he does, closing the door behind him. I root around in the medicine cabinet for a sewing kit and start trying to stitch the bullet wound. I don't know how to suture, so I'm just making a messy stitch, like hemming a pair of pants.

"You ever notice," Randy says quietly, "that all the old zombie movies had happy endings?"

"What?"

"The old movies. The zombie apocalypse. Humanity always died out eventually, and the zombies got to inherit the earth."

"I don't think that was meant to be a happy ending."

He shrugs, and it yanks thread loose. I smack him on the chest. "Sit still. They're going all crooked."

"Sorry."

Silence settles again, the weight of all the things left unsaid.

"It's going to get bad, isn't it?" I ask, finally.

He nods. "Yeah. It's . . . I don't know what'll happen, after. But for a few days, anyway, we're gonna be miserable."

My skin twitches. My body craves the Lazarus like the worst nicotine withdrawal imaginable. The withdrawal, before, was all illness and the creeping awareness of death, the pain that accompanies it. But now, as if my stuttering heart and mangled body know that salvation was within grasp and then snatched away, the craving itself threatens to be unbearable.

"Maybe we'll be okay," Randy says uncertainly.

"You think there's something to what Zoe was saying? About Undead living without Lazarus?"

"No," he replies, with a sigh and a wry smile. His eyes, no longer glittering with smug humor, are dark and somber. "But it'd sure be a nice surprise."

I finish my lopsided suturing, tying off a clumsy knot, and he slides down from the counter where he's been sitting. He starts for the door, turning at the hall as if to leave, and I grab for his arm. "No. Stay."

His brows lift. "You askin' me to stay the night?"

I give him an exasperated look. "I just mean . . . it's been a long night. Tomorrow . . . no, *today*, is going to be . . . God knows what. Just stay, and we'll try to make a plan when it's light out." I realize I'm still holding his arm at the wrist, and loosen my grip. "Sleep wherever you want."

When Randy sleeps, he snores—a deep, terrible choking sound, air compressed through a damaged windpipe. His breath falters often, a strangled gurgle, before righting itself. I can hear him across the hall in the master bedroom, the way I used to lie awake and listen to Dad's cries in the dark.

At least he's sleeping soundly. It's more than I can say for myself. I'm lying in bed, staring up into the darkness, thoughts refusing to loosen their hold. My mind's feeling feverish, agitated, and it jumps from one thought to the next like someone flipping through channels. Behind my eyelids, I can see that feral look on Javier's face, the way his teeth glinted as he bared them. I keep convincing myself that I can hear gunfire; the memory of the sound echoes in my head just as I start to fall asleep, and I jerk awake, mentally wired, physically exhausted.

Morning comes quickly, sunlight edging around the corners of the blackout curtains, and I watch the gray dawn slowly start to fade into bright morning.

I wonder how the others are getting on. Ash and Andrea. Wonder what their loved ones are thinking right now. I try to imagine calling Ash to tell him the news, but just the thought of it exhausts me. I'll need to tell Zoe the story, and I can't imagine telling it twice. Not right now. Not when it takes every bit of energy I have to remember how to breathe, to coordinate my limbs. I'm feeling shivery, feverish.

Whatever happens next will happen soon. Hours, not days. Something's shifting inside my body, some listlessness, some awful squirming feeling. And the more time I spend here worrying, the less time I'll have to prepare.

Exhausted, weary from the sleepless night, I heave myself back out of bed and stumble into the hall. I need to talk to Zoe and Randy. We need to make a plan, while we still have the chance.

"Davin, I already told you—"

"Promise me!"

Zoe looks at me with tired eyes, but she nods. "I promise."

"I'm still not comfortable with you being in the house," I say. I've raised this point already, but the argument goes nowhere, just chases its tail. I don't want Zoe to be here, but I can't think of anywhere for her to go. I could send her to CJ's, but she can't stay there for days. I can't send her to Ash's house, or Jo's; everyone I know is living the same hell that I am.

"Too bad," Zoe says, with a hint of mischief in her smile. "You're stuck with me. Do you need anything before I lock the door?"

Randy's already inside, still curled up in the blankets of Dad's old bed. I think he's pretending to be asleep; he hasn't stirred in a while, but I haven't heard him snoring either. Just as well. It's easier to describe the plan without additional input, anyway.

I'm leaning against the door frame of the master bedroom, clutching it at either side because I'm afraid I'll hit the floor if I don't. I feel like I have the worst flu of my life, but I'm not lucky enough for it just to be the flu.

Everything hurts, and my eyeballs seem likely to burst from their sockets. But that's not the worst part. The worst part is the queasy trembling inside, the feeling that I need to throw up and the awful knowledge that if I do, I might never be able to stop.

Actually, that's the second worst part. The worst is remembering the look in Javier's eyes, the hunger as he lunged for Chuy's throat. Imagining me in his place, slamming Zoe to the ground, tearing into her. Losing myself somehow, even though it doesn't make any sense. None of this has made any sense.

I shake my head, swallowing back bile. It tastes thick and foul, like the black stuff that oozes from roadkill left too long in the sun. I don't trust myself to say anything, to open my mouth, so I pull back from the door and stumble into the room.

Zoe's smile wanes a little, and something flickers behind her thick-rimmed glasses. "It's okay," she says, and I can tell from the glint in her eyes that she believes it. "You'll be fine. I knew the story about Lazarus withdrawal was bullshit."

"Zoe." I swallow. The room seems to sway around us. "I watched someone get their face chewed off last night."

"*After* the guy took Lazarus," she said, dismissive in the way that only someone who wasn't there could be. It's not real to her. It's a hypothetical, the same as the stories on the news, the headlines she pores over and blogs about.

"I don't know what happened. I'm not taking any chances."

She starts to say something, then simply withdraws without a word, shutting the door and locking it behind her. How many times did I lock that door behind myself, imprisoning Dad inside?

How did he feel, waiting out the night in here?

Was it anything like this?

"No matter what," I say now, to the closed door, "don't open the door."

"I'll have to open it eventually to let you out," Zoe says, voice muffled slightly by the thick wood between us.

"I'm not joking around."

"Get some rest, Davin. You look like shit. I'll see you on the other side, I know it."

Over the door frame, dangling awkwardly at the end of a long cord, Zoe's set up a camera, positioned in the corner so it can capture most of the room. The webcam was her idea, obviously. She'd assured me that it would stay private, closed circuit, fed only to her devices.

"So I can monitor what's going on," she'd said, and I have to admit it was a smart idea. It would give her some forewarning if something terrible were happening; would give her a little bit of a head start in case we began to turn.

"And besides," she'd added with that confident look, that trying-to-convince-us-both smile, "when you're both totally fine afterward, we'll have it on tape."

I wish I could share in her confidence.

CHAPTER TWENTY

I MAKE MY way to the bed, where Randy has abandoned his pretenses of sleep. He huddles up against the headboard, watching me. I move to perch on the far end. The air between us is thick with uneasiness.

"This is like the weirdest fucking sleepover," Randy says finally, breaking the silence.

"I don't think I'd know," I say, trying to remember whether I'd ever had a real sleepover. "My dad was a paranoid drunk. Not great for inviting friends over."

Randy grins, but the expression is lifeless. His eyes are glassy, darkened, the way the light goes out of a corpse's eyes. They seem sunken, accentuated by the dark circles beneath that spill over onto his cheekbones. "I couldn't have boys over to stay the night either. My father seemed to think something *inappropriate* might happen."

Our eyes meet, and we laugh, a subdued echo of last night. We're both too exhausted, even for hysteria.

I try to sleep, though I'm not tired. When I close my eyes, I can see things, images that twist around in my semi-consciousness, half-dream and half-memory. They jumble together and make little sense, and when I open my eyes, they're still in the room with me, crowding around and blurring together. I can't tell if I'm dreaming or hallucinating. Nothing feels real anymore, but nothing hurts, and part of me wonders if maybe I've finally truly died, if this is what death is supposed to feel like.

But then that numbness evaporates, as quickly as it had come, and the clenching pain that replaces is it terrible, like being shot through with electricity and hot pokers and cactus needles all at once. It's like my guts have turned to worms and rats, all eager to chew and scratch their way out, and I scream and curse and time ceases to mean anything.

Something inside of me, deep and primal, awakens. It twists and writhes within my body, and I feel with terrible certainty that I'm merely an egg, an incubator for something that's nearly ready to hatch. It beats against the cage of my body and demands release, and I know I'm not strong enough to keep it contained.

The room feels unnaturally dark, even though there's light outside. It's like someone hit a dimmer switch on my vision. My consciousness slowly seems to divorce itself from my body, like a boat that's lost its anchor and begins drifting slowly out to sea. The room twists and distorts around me. I feel untethered.

My body moves of its own accord. I'm only vaguely aware of its actions. I can feel, as if at a great distance, the pounding of my hands against the door, the way my fingers curl like claws. I'm aware of the rough carpet against my cheek as I collapse.

Then I'm aware of nothing but inky blackness.

Senses return one at a time, filling in piecemeal. My body doesn't feel quite right, like my skin is too tight. Like a snake, squirming and coiling as it tries to shed its skin—the dead part of itself, the part that's been outgrown and best left behind.

Snakes. Symbols of renewal. Eternity. Infinity.

But does eternity count for anything if the cycle of life and death is interrupted? There can be no rebirth if you're trapped in purgatory.

I feel calm. That's the part that surprises me. I expected to feel the rage, the hunger. I expected to be a prisoner, taking backseat to some darker impulse. But it doesn't come. I'm still on the far side of waking, lost in darkness, my mind not yet connected completely to my body.

Consciousness, the last of my senses to return; I grapple with it, try to cut through the confusion, to sort out what I'm imagining and what I'm sensing and what I'm thinking.

Randy's talking. I don't think he's talking to me. It's a faraway voice, like he's calling from a long distance, and I yearn toward it. The room is dark, fading to black at the corners—or maybe it's just my vision. It's like there's a spotlight overhead, a light shining down on me, creating an island of illumination. Everything outside of the golden illuminated circle is nothing. Void. Emptiness.

Death.

Something about this feels familiar. Like I've been here before.

But my island isn't the only one, and I crawl toward the other pinpoint of light. I grab at the mattress, pulling myself up onto the bed with some effort, a snake slithering upward.

Randy's voice starts to make sense, sounds turning into words. He's huddled against the headboard, sitting up now, body drawn close and small as defense against the darkness. Tears, tinged with blood, streak down either side of his pale face. Stigmata.

My stomach bucks, threatening a purge, and I retch. But there's nothing inside. The coughing comes up empty.

"I tried to kill myself twice," Randy's saying, and his voice is far away, robotic. Dead, like his eyes. The sound of a voice on a tape recording. "The third time I actually did it. And somehow I still fucked it all up."

I try to get closer to him, but it's like the bed is an insurmountable expanse. It twists and writhes beneath me, and as I pull myself forward it retreats, broadening the gap between us.

"It wasn't depression. I just wanted that bastard to pay. For him to hurt a little. Feel something. For once in his goddamn life, to pay attention."

He doesn't seem to notice me; his eyes don't stray in my direction.

"He was always campaigning, you know? Always putting on a good face for the voters. And there I was, the embarrassment, the fuckup, the shameful son. Kissing boys and getting busted at parties and racking up misdemeanors. Just stupid shit. Just to get under his skin . . . "

He falls silent, and something passes over his face, features rearranging themselves into a stormy glower, a grimace of pain.

I inch closer. I feel like he must be nearby now; I think I can feel his weight in the tension on the blankets. So why does he still feel so far away?

"You know it was the goddamn maid who found me? I hung myself from the banister over the living room. First thing you'd see when you come through the door. I did it on purpose, y'know? So he'd see me and feel something."

Another wave of pain, a cramp, runs through my gut and I double over. For a moment, time slips away from me again. When I get hold of myself again, he's still talking; I don't know how much I've missed, whether it was a moment or an hour or if time even means anything anymore.

"He was out late that night. Never even came home. Probably fucking somebody, for all I know. But I woke up. It must have been hours. Still just hanging there, all by myself, helpless. Couldn't even get myself down."

I reach out. My hand touches something solid, and I grasp for it, pulling myself closer.

"You know what I thought? I thought, this is hell. They were right all along, those Bible study bastards. You kill yourself, and hell is waking up to realize that nothing's fucking changed. Hell is realizing that there's no way out. The maid found me and cut me down. And you know the worst part? Dad was pissed. After all that, the only thing he felt was disappointed."

His hand clenches into a fist, and I realize that it's gripping mine, so I squeeze back. I lean into him. He's cool to the touch; but then, so am I.

"All I wanted was to see him grieve," Randy's saying, and his voice is down to a rasping whisper. "Just feel sad. Be sorry. But instead, I was just a new kind of embarrassment."

I can't speak. There's nothing to say, even if I could.

I pull in close, and he presses against me and lays his head against my chest.

We sleep like the dead.

Zombies get their happy ending at the end of the world.

Randy was right all along, the apocalypse is the beginning of their story. I never used to think about zombies, but now I can't help but wonder. When they stumble and moan their way through life, are they aware? Are they trapped inside their brains, held hostage as their bodies betray them—force them to eat flesh, to gnaw bones?

Does it hurt them the way it hurts me?

They're always the bad guys. The last humans we're allowed to hate; the humans we're allowed to kill. Video games and movies and television, glorifying their gory demise; violence against them justified by their brutishness, their emptiness. Nothing but hungry vessels.

Or maybe that's just what people have to tell themselves to get by.

All this time, I thought I'd lose myself. I never imagined I might be imprisoned, held hostage, instead of transformed. The idea could never have occurred to me before, not when it was so much easier to draw clean lines between good and evil, safety and danger.

But the lines are all blurred now, erased like so much chalk, and all that's left behind are people: two bodies held in an embrace, like skeletons in the ruins of Pompeii.

CHAPTER TWENTY-ONE

THE SOUND OF BIRDS.
Quiet, at first, then insistent and growing louder. Deafening, almost, amplified like a hangover. It sounds like there must be a million of them out there.

It's light out. Morning—bright. Dad's window, not shrouded by a blackout curtain, allows the light to stream in uninhibited. The sun streams in onto the bed, the beam lazy and golden, like a shaft of light over a tomb.

Randy's still leaning against my chest. He's stopped trembling, and so have I.

Aside from the chirping outside, everything is silent, perfectly still; the stillness of a snowy morning. The stillness of rebirth. Of coming back to life.

"We're okay," Randy says, mumbling it against my chest. He sounds incredulous.

Everything hurts—that much hasn't changed. But it's a different sort of pain. A distant, numbing ache, not the terrible agony of the hours before. A manageable sort of pain.

"How long do you think it's been?" I finally ask, trying to sense every inch of my body, assess every limb without moving. I'm afraid that if I do move, the agony will come back—as if the only thing keeping it at bay is my stillness, Randy's proximity, the shared nightmare of the struggle that drew us together here.

"No telling," he says, and makes no move to get up. He seems exhausted.

It's morning, but which morning? Has it been one day, or many? Is there a world outside of this room, a world that doesn't smell like decay, that isn't painted in blood and the vile fluids of death? It's hard to believe that. It's hard to believe that anything exists after what we've been through, a crucible that would be impossible to explain to anyone who hadn't survived it themselves.

"I . . . don't think it's going to happen," Randy says finally. He pushes himself upright, hesitantly leaving the nest he'd made for himself against my side.

I don't have to ask him what he means. The same thought's crowding my mind, the only thing I can really make sense of now.

The room is a mess. It looks like a crime scene, with blood and other fluids staining the bedding, the carpet, the walls. Things are torn that I don't remember tearing. A pillow is unstuffed, bits of poly-fill scattered like snow all over the room. There are deep scratches in the wall at the head of the bed.

I don't remember doing any of this, but there's a lot of time left unaccounted for.

"I think . . . maybe the Dusty Bones were right," I say. "And I don't know what that means."

I'm fine. We're both fine. It was terrible, but it's over, and now here we are.

"I can't think about it right now," Randy says, and rolls out of the bed, stumbling, catches himself. He stands uneasily, wobbling like his legs are asleep. "That's the bathroom, right?"

I nod. He gingerly makes his way across the bedroom toward the master bath, and I can see the way his shirt clings to him: plastered to his skin from feverish sweat, matted to the wound in his side. He grabs the edges and pulls it up, peeling it from him, like a snake shedding its skin.

"The camera," I say, suddenly bashful. "My sister is . . . "

"Then come in here," he says, lingering in the doorway of the bathroom. "Where she can't see."

It feels natural, somehow, that we would end up here this way. Together.

The water is as hot as I can stand, nearly scalding, and the room fills quickly with steam. The master bath is bigger than Ash's, without the hollowness under the floor, but the moment is familiar. Coming full circle, the snake that eats its tail.

Dirt and blood and filth strip from our skins, mingling as the water swirls down the drain. It's a tight fit in the shower, but I don't mind.

"You ever hear about the Love Bridge?" Randy is asking me. His fingertips are on my flesh, gently probing at the old wounds there—the patches of skin torn away from my own bloody clothing, skin that tore the day we met. "There's this idea that two people passing on a suspension bridge will fall in love. That the fear of being on the bridge will speed up their hearts, and they'll mistake the fear for love."

I think: *There's been so much fear these last few days. Weeks.* Fear is the white space that encircles the shape of my existence, since the withdrawals . . . since my death . . . since before my death.

I say, "Are you trying to tell me something?"

His eyes have lost that glassy quality, the sheen of life returning to them. They're depthless pools, eyes you can get lost in.

He tilts his head back to look up at me, and our height difference strikes me as if for the first time. So many times now, he's been the one leaning over me—the one who saves me. It's only now that I realize how small he is, how vulnerable.

I wonder what he remembers. If he knows the secret he told me.

My fingers move of their own volition, gently brushing the sides of his neck, tracing over the dark bruise at his throat. Then my hands are in his hair, and his lips lightly part as I lean forward and cover his mouth with mine and for a moment, in the warmth of the shower, the water beating down against us, our bodies melding together, hands traveling against skin and fingers grasping, encircling, stroking—for a moment, it almost feels like I'm alive.

CHAPTER TWENTY-TWO

WE REALIZE, TOO late, that we have no fresh clothes. There are towels, however, and I fish a pair of them out of the cabinet. They're musty from storage, and I shake them out, checking for spiders, before handing one to Randy. I wrap the other around my waist and start for the bedroom door, walking gingerly over the messy carpet. The room is trashed. It'll take ages to clean it up, but just now I don't even mind.

I pause at the door, listening for Zoe. There's no movement outside, no sounds of life. I lean against the door, straining to hear a television, a radio, the click of a keyboard, the buzzing of a phone—anything. But it's deathly quiet outside, and my temporary peace begins to shake loose. I can only feel the exhilaration of survival for so long before the reality of circumstance comes once more.

I try the doorknob. Locked. I knock on the door. "Zoe?"

Nothing.

I glance over my shoulder at Randy, shooting him a questioning look. He's at the bedroom window, assessing the wrought-iron burglar bars from the inside like he's contemplating breaking out. I turn again to the door, knock again, louder and more insistently. "Zoe?"

A rustle. A confused noise, like someone waking up. And then, quietly, "Davin?"

"Yeah. Uh." I look up at the camera poised over the door, and wave at it, awkwardly.

Silence. Then another rustle, and the sound of the lock popping open.

Zoe's glasses are askew and dirty, smeared. Her eyes are red-rimmed and puffy, and a flush has spread over her nose and cheeks. There's a sleeping bag and pillow on the floor in the hall outside the bedroom, her cell phone and a few books and notebooks scattered where she's been camping. Nesting outside the door.

She hesitates in the doorway, peering inside. Looking past me to Randy, both of us dripping and wrapped in faded old towels. Then to the room around us, the crime-scene disaster of it. Her eyes widen, and before I even see her move she's hugging me, wrapping her arms around tight and burying her face into my still-damp chest. I freeze, awkward, holding my towel in place with one hand while I try to comfort her with the other.

"I thought you were dead," she says. A pause. Then, exasperated, "I mean . . . You know what I mean."

I scoot forward, trying to extricate myself so we can get out of the doorway. Zoe finally relents, letting go and retreating back, opening the path across the hall to my bedroom. I nod for Randy to go first. "Help yourself to anything in there," I say, "if you can find something that fits."

"How are you?" Zoe asks as Randy enters my room.

"I feel . . . good, actually," I say, and realize as I say it that it's true. The pain is present, but muted. The hollow ache in my gut persists, but compared to the searing agony of withdrawal, I can hardly feel it. But the surprising thing is how steady I feel on my feet. There's no trembling in my extremities, no tingling in my fingertips, and my tired dead heart beats a steady, quiet rhythm. I lift my hand to my ribs and lay it over my heart, and marvel for a moment at the lack of pain in my chest. "Have you heard from the others?"

"Jo dropped in a few times with food. I think she was afraid I wouldn't eat otherwise." Zoe manages to roll her eyes, for the sake of her image, but it's clear that she was pleased with the company. "I guess Andrea's doing okay. Lilith just sent an email a while ago. Ash is fine. Everyone made it through okay."

"No rage?"

She shakes her head. "Not really, I guess. Nobody's given me a lot of details. It sounded awful. There was so much screaming. But nobody's . . . you know."

"A zombie?" There's something she's not saying, something that's bothering her. "How long has it been?"

"Two days," she says, and her voice cracks a little. "You guys stopped screaming last night. I was afraid that . . . well. It was hard to make anything out on the camera. I wish we'd thought to put night vision on it or something. Especially now that we know."

I try to smile. "To be fair, we were working on a tight schedule."

Zoe doesn't echo my smile, and that makes me uncomfortable. She's acting weird. I was expecting relief, certainly, but also an "I told you so."

I drop my voice, glancing at my door. "What's up?"

"I told you. There's no footage." Her eyes lift, meeting mine, and I can see the maelstrom of emotions fighting for dominance across her features—a face that can't decide whether to cry or scream or smile. "We know, now, for sure, what happens when you go off the Lazarus. We know that the media's been lying. And there's no way for us to prove it."

My bedroom door opens, and Randy appears. He's wearing one of my dress shirts; it hangs well past his hips, and the open top button sags down past his collarbone. But it's clean, at least, and the old gym shorts he's found fit well enough. "See, now, Zoe, that's where you're wrong," he says, and looks over her head to meet my eyes. "Maybe we can't prove it yet. But we know the truth, the whole lot of us. And you can't know a truth this big without it getting out eventually."

I mutter my agreement, and I'm glad to see the change in Zoe's expression—the light of hope that returns to her eyes. But I'm not feeling it. All I can feel, right now, is relief—and exhaustion. Weariness. And an odd, quiet sort of contentment. Let them fight their good fight. Let them shine a light on the truth.

Somebody has to.

But for myself, I'm satisfied just to have survived.

I head into my room, choosing clothes at random. Then I get in bed, collapsing into it and allowing myself to sleep, for the first time in a long while, without fear or nightmares or convoluted fever dreams. When I awaken, hours later, Zoe's in her room, the red light bulb lit above her door. The sound of keys, business as usual, her convictions renewed. Randy's still here, curled up on the couch, half-watching an old black-and-white movie on the TV. It's *Night of the Living Dead*.

"We win," he says, tilting his head to look up at me sidelong.

"For now," I agree. "For now, we win."

ABOUT THE AUTHOR

T.L. Bodine is the author of *INSOMNIA: Stories to Read with the Lights Turned On* and the Wattpad-exclusive *The Hound.* As a writer, she's interested in uncanny, fantastic things, and the way normal people interact with them. She lives near Albuquerque, New Mexico with her husband and two small dogs. You can find her online at tlbodine.tumblr.com, where she posts creepy flash fiction and keeps tabs on the indie horror community.

www.ingramcontent.com/pod-product-compliance
Lightning Source LLC
LaVergne TN
LVHW050134210225
803812LV00001B/33